WATERMELON FALL

WATERMELON FALL

Robert W. West

To my favorite dentist!

Robert W West

iUniverse, Inc.

New York Lincoln Shanghai

WATERMELON FALL

Copyright © 2005 by Robert W. West

iUniverse books may be ordered through booksellers or by contacting:

iUniverse
2021 Pine Lake Road, Suite 100
Lincoln, NE 68512
www.iuniverse.com
1-800-Authors (1-800-288-4677)

ISBN-13: 978-0-595-35603-4 (pbk)
ISBN-13: 978-0-595-67242-4 (cloth)
ISBN-13: 978-0-595-80084-1 (ebk)
ISBN-10: 0-595-35603-6 (pbk)
ISBN-10: 0-595-67242-6 (cloth)
ISBN-10: 0-595-80084-X (ebk)

Printed in the United States of America

To the late, Dr. William L. White, director of, The Julia and David White Artists' Colony, in Ciudad Colon, Costa Rica. May your work be continued. I thank you once again, Bill. Sorry you didn't make it.

ACKNOWLEDGMENTS

I wish to thank three very important women in my life (names withheld) who, each in her own way, inspired me to write this story.

To my five daughters, Rolinda, Sabrina, Yolanda, Helena and Amanda; thank you for helping to fill the pages of my *Book of Life* and for giving my life a reason and a purpose.

I thank William Shakespeare, Edmond Rostand, Henry Wadsworth Longfellow, and Kahlil Gibran for writing such powerful words of love and endearment, a few of which I have borrowed for this novel. I would also like to thank Rachmaninoff for his beautiful and inspiring music. His music kept me at the computer keyboard and helped me intensify my love story.

My gratitude is extended to Georgia Southern University and the town of Statesboro, Georgia, for the memories and visions of the glorious seventies. I still carry them within my heart. A few of them are shared with the readers of this story.

My deepest appreciation goes out to Dr. William L. White, director of The Julia and David White Artists' Colony located in Ciudad Colon, Costa Rica, for accepting me as one of their artist fellows and for providing me with a sanctuary away from the unrelenting stimuli of the modern world for an entire month. The silence, the breathtaking beauty of the surroundings, the magnificence of the flora and fauna, the one intrusive sound (but nevertheless beautiful unto itself) of the ringing of the local cathedral bells early in the morning and evening gave me

viii   WATERMELON FALL

the power to finish the first draft of this novel in two and a half weeks. Thanks again, Bill, and may your dreams for the colony be realized.

My appreciation must also be offered to my fantastic editor, Ms. Marcella Sherman. Without her contributions this novel would never have been written.

PROLOGUE

▼

Dad, wherever you might be and whatever form you're in, this book is for you. It's not the empirical research book that you so wanted to write during your lifetime. It is, however, your and mother's love story, a story that embodies a large part of what love is, or should be. And love is the idea or concept that you spent your entire academic life pursuing. You might say that this story comes from the heart itself: yours, Mom's, and mine. I have drawn together notes, not only from your historical research and manuscript, but from your personal diary. This love story that you and Mom created will lift both of you from the world of obscurity to the world of immortality, with, of course, a little help from your daughter.

You once mentioned to Mother that the more educated you became, the more you were convinced that you were a major part of the construct making up the universe and that Jesus Christ was your one and only hero. So, whether you are in heaven or floating around in some form of molecular structure, I'm sure that you are aware that this daughter graduated from your Alma Mater, Boston University with a major in English and a concentration in creative writing. My first objective following graduation was to write this novel. In writing it, I knew that I would have you and Mom with me always. You know that Mother gave her last breath of life on the delivery table when I entered this world. I would like to believe that both of you, in whatever form, are now together for eternity.

You should be quite proud of my sisters. Regina retired from the Army with the rank of full colonel and gave birth to one son. When she was in the Orient, she adopted a beautiful baby girl. Salina is president of her own company and mother of four wonderful children, and little Theresa is now an outstanding RN and mother of two. You started a dynasty. You are remembered and loved by all of us.

CHAPTER 1

▼

"'Tis better to have loved and lost than never to have loved at all."

—Alfred Lord Tennyson

Crack! Crack! The sound filled the room as solid colored balls began to disappear from the table. Will's study, bar, and game room were wall-to-wall mahogany. The pool table occupied a major portion of the game room. Its eminent presence in the room was shared only by four deer hunting trophies hanging on the wall. The bar and study area were carpeted in deep purple, Will's favorite color. The floor of the game room had had to be compromised because of the children. The French doors led out to the swimming pool; as a consequence, the game room had a blue indoor/outdoor carpet for wet exits and entrances. Will wanted to change this once his children left the nest.

Will's special guest for the day was one of his closest and dearest friends, Professor Mark Phillips. A very important contest was in progress. Mark was sitting at the bar while Will was preparing a shot at the eight ball. Two of Will's teenaged children were outside enjoying the pool.

Mark stared into his scotch and soda glass. The fresh ice cubes took on the appearance of Austrian crystal. He lifted his glass in the gesture of a toast and softly quoted:

"It is wrong to think that love comes from long companionship and persevering courtship. Love is the offspring of spiritual affinity, and unless that affinity is created in a moment, it will not be created in years or even generations."

Will took his shot at the eight ball with hopes of sinking it into the right corner pocket.

"And…" There was a long pause. Will continued, "Am I your sounding board again?"

"Well…" said Mark.

"It sounded pretty good, Mark. Another piece of research for your book?"

Mark looked up from his perspiring glass. "You guessed it. In fact, the author of that quote is a man after my own heart."

Will took another shot at the eight ball, "Might I ask who in the hell are you talking about?"

"The author of those words came from the country of Lebanon. His name, Kahlil Gibran. Any book on the subject of love would be an empty shell if some of his thoughts were not included. It would be like leaving out quotations from the Bible or forgetting what William Shakespeare had to say about love and romance. Didn't you ever come across him in college or maybe in med school?"

Will looked up from the pool table. "Are you going to spend another Saturday attempting to educate me about love, or are you going to play me a game of pool? And…if you finish that scotch, which will be about your eighth, you might not even be able to spot the balls on the table. When I have you over, my scotch bill starts looking like the national debt." Mark placed his glass very carefully on top of the bar, and like a mummy rising up from a coffin, stood and tramped to the pool table. Placing his hands on the table, he leaned towards Will, who was on the opposite side. "Are you going to give me a breathalyzer test, Doc?" Mark straightened, "You know the only reason you set up this yearly adventure and provide me with all the barbecue I can eat and all the scotch I can hold is I'm the only, I repeat, the only, friend you have who isn't worth shit when it comes to hitting those defenseless balls with a stick. I've never been good at any sport involving spherical balls. This includes golf, tennis, soccer, basketball, volleyball, etc. You will be advised, however…" Mark picked up one of the billiard balls and rolled it around in his hand, "That a football is not round; it is not a sphere. In that sport, I excelled. Played it all through high school and two years in the U. S. Marines. In fact, Doctor William Westmore, I had the opportunity to play foot-ball on a college scholarship when I left the Corps." Mark gently placed the bil-liard ball back on the table and chalked the end of his cue stick, and crossed slowly around to the back of Will. He spoke softly over Will's shoulder. "If those balls on this table were shaped like footballs, I would have no problem tossing the eight ball into any pocket I chose." With that comment, Mark paused to catch his breath and said with a bit of bravado, "Rack 'em, Westmore!" Their yearly, late spring ritual in the small college town of Magnolia, Georgia, was about to begin.

Magnolia was the twin to just about any small town located in the South. In the town square, of any county seat, is a county court house, and in front of the court house, a bronze statue of a Confederate soldier, sometimes standing but, most of the time, on a horse. The soldier's shoulders are white from the adulation of the local pigeon population. Surrounding the square is the business district, and outside of the business district, which stretches out from the square about five or six blocks in either direction, are farm land and farm houses. As in quite a few small Southern towns, there are always a few businesses springing up here and there. In Magnolia, tobacco was king. Warehouses, drying houses, and auction barns were numerous. A plant that produced rubber products was located a few miles from the center of town. The last major business of importance was Northeast Georgia State University.

During the summer, Magnolia's population numbered seventeen thousand residents; in the fall, its population increased by eight to nine thousand inhabitants. Magnolia was blessed in its geographical location. It rested in a valley, surrounded by the small mountains that make up the lower portion of the Appalachian Mountain chain. The locals called them hills, and the people from the flatlands called them mountains. Mountains or hills, in the spring and fall of the year, they became God's works of art. The town was further blessed with a beautiful river which ran along the northern edge of the county, turned south to gently flow within two miles west of the city limits. A small creek, where the river took a southern turn, moved aimlessly to the campus of NGSU and formed a rather nice-sized lake on the west side of the university. The grassy area fronting the lake was an ideal spot for outdoor spring classes and late-night, romantic rendezvous. During mid to late spring, around the edges of the lake, color exploded like the colors of skyrockets on the Fourth of July when hundreds of azalea bushes burst into bloom.

In the early spring of 1964, Professor Mark Phillips came to NGSU for his initial interview. The faculty members and administrators who interviewed Mark were quite impressed with him and his credentials, especially the numerous professional publications. Being published, and the more often the merrier, for any professor is as important to career advancement as is the measurements of 36-24-36 to a nightclub stripper.

Upon his first visit to the NGSU campus, Mark thought he had set foot in the wrong area of the country. The buildings on campus were covered with ivy. The fertile ground in and around the university provided the ideal soil for the growth of just about anything, and the weather, especially during the winter months, came close to the same kind of weather found in the lower New England area. The intervals of winter were shorter, yet they were similar to those found around the Ivy League towers of higher education. Consequently, Mark Phillips, for a few brief hours, felt as though he was walking around the ivy-covered towers and walkways of Harvard University. Mark did have a fantastic imagination. Not only was he overawed with the campus, he immediately fell in love with the colorful brilliance of the blooming azaleas surrounding the campus lake. Mark was a romantic, and Magnolia, Georgia, with mountains for a backdrop, and the beauty of the NGSU campus, was a romantic setting. It was much more romantic than the surroundings of Dillard University in New Orleans.

When Mark graduated with his PhD in English from Boston University in 1960, not many institutions of higher learning were interested in hiring new instructors. He was offered four jobs, two of them from colleges in the desert southwest, one small college in the hills of Tennessee, and Dillard University, in party town New Orleans. The city and its history fascinated Mark. He was also intrigued by the fact that Dillard was primarily an all-Black institution. Its roots extended to the years just following the Civil War. Dillard, New Orleans, the mighty Mississippi, and Dixieland Jazz held a romantic allure for the young professor. Mark accepted Dillard's offer and began his first assignments as an instructor, teaching four classes of English Composition and one Creative Writing course.

The years at Dillard University were tumultuous years of change, not only in the life of Mark Phillips (his third daughter, Theresa, was born in 1962) but in the history of America. John F. Kennedy, was assassinated, his brother Bobby Kennedy was killed; Martin Luther King, Jr., was executed, and the Viet Nam War was quite active, with the blood of Americans and Vietnamese fertilizing the jungles. The last year of Mark's tenure at Dillard saw the passing of the Civil Rights Act and the first Freedom March in the history of New Orleans. Mark took part. Along with thousands of his black and white brothers, sisters, students, and co-workers, he marched from Shakespeare Park to the front steps of the New Orleans City Hall where they joined hands and together, in one voice, sang out, "We shall overcome some day." Mark later talked often of this event. He was proud to have been part of that history; however, he always ended his conversation with, "God must have been deaf that particular evening. I don't think he heard our voices. I know the politicians didn't."

Dr. Will had just missed his call shot on the eight ball. It was now Mark's turn on the green felt field. Mark had one solid-color ball remaining on the table. If he sunk it with this shot, it would finally be his turn to name his pocket for the black ball.

Tension was mounting. Mark had never been this close to winning a pool game with Dr. Will since they started their little spring tournament over ten years ago. The cue stick slid back and forth through his fingers like a piston moving through warm grease. He took aim at the remaining solid-color ball, and with a resounding crack of the stick striking the cue ball, the solid-color ball went into its destined pocket. Only the black eight ball and the white cue ball remained on the table.

Almost twelve years ago, in mid-summer 1964, Professor Mark Phillips, his family, and a twenty-six-foot long U-Haul pulled into the foothills of the Tray Mountains in Georgia. During his previous visit to Magnolia, in the midst of signing contracts and meeting his colleagues, Mark found a nice, three-bedroom, ranch-style home just outside the city limits that he felt would be perfect for his family. He had been made aware that all public schools were serviced by school buses that traversed the entire county, making sure that no county school resident was left out of obtaining an education. A few chain grocery stores were within a few miles of the house, along with a good-size mall; all of the ingredients that make for a happy wife. The house was a rental, and because it took seven years before anyone was considered for tenure at NGSU, Mark felt that renting until that security was achieved was the best approach.

The Phillips clan had been in Magnolia for only three days when Mark, removing the family refrigerator from the U-Haul, slipped with the dolly and its load as he attempted to descend the unloading ramp. Instantly, he tore a few back muscles as his body met the ground. Gloria, Mark's wife, immediately called another professor's wife and asked for the closest doctor's office. She also asked about the closest hospital. Mark walked in on the phone call to inform his wife that he didn't need to go to any hospital but that a doctor would do and so would some good, strong pain medication.

Off they went to the nearest doctor's office, the office of Dr. William Westmore. The receptionist at the front desk looked rather stunned when she saw Mark sitting in the waiting room. Gloria pointed to her husband and told the receptionist that he was in a great deal of pain and needed to see the doctor right away. The receptionist, wide-eyed and seemingly in shock, replied with a "Yes, ma' am!" and quickly disappeared down the hall. Within seconds, Dr. Westmore was standing in the waiting room looking down on a moaning, groaning, Professor Mark Phillips. Mark was looking at the floor, and Gloria was doing her best to rub out some of his discomfort.

"Are you sure you are at the right doctor's office, Mr. Phillips?"

Without looking up, Mark replied, "If you are a medical doctor, I'm at the right office. If you're a veterinarian…well, I still might be in the right place," and Mark let out a long groan. He could see the white coat in front of him and slowly but painfully raised his head and looked into the eyes of Dr. Westmore.

"You will have to forgive me, Mr. Phillips, if I seem to be in somewhat of a stupor, but you are the first white patient in the history of my practice here in Magnolia....Are you sure you're in the right place?"

Mark didn't so much as blink at the comment made by Dr. Westmore. He'd just left New Orleans and Dillard University where, his friends and colleagues were black. However, even with his pain, he was amused at the look on the doctor's face.

"Dr. Westmore, if you can take away some of the pain in my back, I will make you a solemn promise that I will not be the last white patient to enter your office." He looked into the face and eyes of a caring doctor of medicine. Westmore's smile was warm and genuine. That moment launched an enduring friendship.

Mark slowly raised the cue stick into position. He moved it slowly back and forth between his raised thumb and balancing forefinger. "One good, direct hit on that cue ball," thought Mark, "and this game will be mine." His concentration was intense as he pulled back on his cue stick for the strike.

"Hey, Dad!" shouted Calvin to Will as he rushed through the patio doors. He stood dripping wet. Directly behind him, adding to the water puddle on the game room floor, was his twin sister, Tanya.

Mark's concentration flew out the open French doors.

Will was doing his best to contain an explosive laugh at the frustrated expression on Mark Phillips face. It resembled a white prune. "Yes, son?"

"As you know, Dad, today is our senior skip day."

"I'm with you. So?"

"The rec center is holding a special senior's party, and Tanya and I would like to go."

"You have my blessing, providing you first towel up that pond you and your sister have created on the floor of my game room."

"Thanks, Dad. Tanya and I will scrape up some towels and be right back."

Calvin looked at Professor Phillips, and with a parting smile said, "Forgive us for interrupting your game." They disappeared as quickly as they'd appeared.

"Sorry about the intrusion," Will said with a smile on his face, "You were about to win your first game of pool since we started playing twelve years ago."

Mark shook his head, laughed, and said, "I think you set the whole thing up."

Laughing with Mark, Will continued, "The winning possibility still exists. Make your shot, Professor Phillips!"

Mark once again, took his position on the side of the pool table and began slowly moving the cue stick through his fingers…the cue stick suddenly stilled, and Mark straightened.

"I do believe I'll wait until the mop squad returns." Both men continued their laughter as they walked over to the bar. Mark mixed up a scotch and soda, and Will popped the top of another beer.

Mark slid onto the bar stool, took a quick sip of his drink, and looked at Will. He opened his mouth as if to speak but didn't.

"I take it, Mark, that you were preparing to ask me a question?"

"As a matter of fact I was."

"Well, out with it. You're sitting on that stool, looking at me as if someone just, shot a cork into your mouth."

"To tell you the truth, I don't know the correct way to start talking about the subject. However, I'll start off with a curved ball approach."

"Well, I hope you will use a football! In the meantime, I don't know what in the hell you want to talk about, Mark, but having known you for going on thirteen years, I've become accustomed to some of your thought processes. Especially when you've had a few."

"Didn't you tell me once upon a time, I think it was during one of our lunches at the Inn, that you were originally from New Jersey?"

"Yes."

"And, you did your residency at Johns Hopkins University?"

"Yes."

"And that you met Gail, your wife, in Atlanta during some kind of medical convention?"

"You're scoring a hundred percent so far, Dr. Phillips."

"Gail was born right here in Magnolia?"

"Well, close enough to be called a native of this fair town."

"Something about this town since I moved here almost twelve years ago from Louisiana has piqued my curiosity, and I believe you are the one person who can put my inquiring mind to rest."

Will's curiosity had been aroused, "May I be so bold as to ask you what all of this has to do with Gail or me?"

"When I was teaching at Dillard, I was introduced to many different segments of the black race, such as mulattos, octaroons, quadroons, and I'm sure there are other *roons.*" Mark moved awkwardly off the bar stool, "You once told me that Gail was a mulatto and that when you first met her in Atlanta, you thought she was white."

Will smiled, knowing that Mark was getting close to the question that he wanted to ask. He had an idea that the question had to do with race because Mark always became a bit evasive and non-directional when the topic became the center of conversation.

"I did mention that fact to you a few years back." Will thought that he would have some fun with Mark's awkwardness, so he made a quick change of subject.

"Mark, I hate to change the subject, but you haven't been in the office for your yearly physical. In fact, you're way overdue." Will smiled again and waited for Mark's reply.

"I'm on a roll here, Will, and you just threw a railroad tie across my tracks. I'll make an appointment this week." Mark took another sip of his drink and was about to speak but was interrupted by Will.

"That's what you said a couple of weeks ago."

"I'll make a deal with you. Answer the question, and I'll be in your office next week."

Will knew his friend was lying, but the question was also begging his curiosity, so he relinquished the floor.

"Okay, Mark. What's been bothering you all these years?"

"I've noticed over the past twelve years a greater population of light-skinned blacks in this area of Georgia than I saw while in New Orleans. Why?"

"You've been spending all your research time searching for a definition of love in the annals of history as well as in world literature, and none in searching out the history of the town you live in. So, Mr. Professor, I will attempt to enlighten you about your adopted home town." Will took another beer from the refrigerator and gestured to Mark. "You may want to refresh your drink. The story I'm going to tell you will take a few minutes."

Mark sat back on the bar stool. "Try to give it to me in as brief a synopsis as possible. I don't want to let my hot streak cool."

"Hot streak? Will broke into a laugh and continued, "You do know that most of the native population of Magnolia and the area around it is half Yankee and half Southerner?"

"Explain," Mark said with a quizzical look. "And I'm waiting to hear how that remark relates to my question."

"What I am going to tell you is somewhat based in fact and the rest on hand-me-down storytelling…"

"Go on, I'm listening."

"The answer to your question will take us back to the Civil War and, specifically, the spring of 1864."

Calvin and Tanya once again invaded Will's sanctuary. They rushed through the patio doors. Each carried three or four large pool towels and started absorbing the puddle of water they had left behind. While stomping on the towels, Calvin told his Dad he and Tonya needed to hurry and get ready for the party at the rec center. They didn't want to miss the Kiss look-alike contest. The flurry of activity ended as fast as it had begun. The patio door closed. Their laughter and giggles could still be heard as they scurried off to get changed into their party clothes.

Will shook his head and let out a little chuckle. "To be young again. Have you ever entertained a desire to return to your teen years, Mark?" Will turned toward Mark and saw frustration written all over his face.

"Okay, okay, I'll continue from where we were so lovingly interrupted. In the spring of 1864, the town of Magnolia and the surrounding area was sorely bereft of males. Any male big enough to carry a rifle and/or fire one was serving under General Joseph E. Johnston at Rocky Face Ridge in an effort to defeat the approaching Union Army under the command of the infamous—ask any Southerner—General William T. Sherman. The Confederates lost, but the casualties inflicted on the Union soldiers were very high. Consequently, a large number of disillusioned Union soldiers decided that they had had enough of war and decided to head on home. Desert, in other words. A good-sized group of yanks, probably equaling out to a company or platoon strong, moved into this area. Apparently, they were very hungry and very horny. They stripped the area of all the food they could eat or carry and raped every woman they could find. Color was no obstacle. The rest is history."

"My God!" Mark said. "Some of the stories of history that never get printed in the history books!"

Will left the bar and moved toward the pool table.

"You've just learned a bit of local history. It is now time for you to make some history." He gestured toward the pool table. "And here is your field of battle."

Mark slid off of the stool and crossed to the pool table. He picked up his cue stick, grabbed a chalk cube, and began to chalk the end of his stick.

"I'm a bit stunned over the historical information and the answer to my question."

Will reached across the pool table and gently touched the cue ball. "Remember what I have told you or hopefully taught you. You've got an easy shot to wrap up this game. Hit the cue ball directly in the center. A hit or contact on either side of the ball may cause your eight ball to miss the corner pocket. A direct hit is necessary."

"I'll swear, for a M.D., you sure know a helluva lot about pool!"

"How do you think I paid my way through medical school?"

Mark bent over the pool table, positioned his cue stick, and started the aiming process.

"By the way, Mark, I forgot to ask how your bachelor life was progressing. Your second year anniversary is coming up this summer, if I'm not mistaken."

"My bachelor life is developing and getting better with each year. And your estimate of my emancipation anniversary is correct. And now, if you don't mind, I would appreciate total silence while I, as you said, make a little history here this evening."

Mark concentrated on the challenge at hand. His eyes focused on the center of the cue ball, and the cue stick moved slowly and accurately through his fingers. A loud, ear-splitting crack broke the silence in the game room. Mark had declared the corner pocket as target for his eight ball, and that is exactly where it went. Mark let out a shout of victory, and Will gave him a round of applause.

"Your first win in twelve years, Professor."

Will walked around the table to shake the hand of the winner. As he did so, he said, "This might sound crazy, Mark, but I have a strange premonition that even greater moments await you before 1976 passes into history. One of them is getting a clean bill of health when you stop into my office for your physical!"

CHAPTER 2

▼

"Like the measles, love is most dangerous when it comes late in life."

—George Gordon

The azalea bushes surrounding the NGSU lake had dropped their blossoms. It was mid-May and mid-season for azaleas. The petals lay on the ground in large puddles of color. The scene resembled a huge artist's palette. The colors of red, yellow, purple, white, and even the light color of blue seemed to be calling out for one more chance at blinding an audience with their hues, but, like the students, once the final paper has been submitted or the final exam taken, there is no second chance.

The end of the spring semester was just two weeks away. Most classes were in the throes of wrap-up lectures, reviews for final exams, and discussions over final papers. The early morning dew still lingered in the grass. The campus was as quiet as a ghost town lost somewhere in the mountains of Colorado. The solitude was suddenly broken by a lone student crossing campus. His new Marantz Superscope boom box sat on his shoulder and rested against his ear. It was blaring forth the lyrics and melody of "Disco Duck" for all within hearing distance to hear and appreciate, providing one appreciated his selection of music.

In the distance, one of the university's oldest structures stood out from all the rest, the one building on campus that looked like a gigantic pot of ivy. It rose three stories above the ground and was literally covered with climbing ivy from the ground to its rooftop. It was constructed during the early years of the school's history and was the main academic building providing all of the "Normal School" classrooms. Today, it was the Humanities building, its classrooms were devoted to English and Literature, Journalism, History, Visual Arts, Music, Dance, and Theatre Arts. One of the windows on the second floor was open. Closed blinds covered the window cavity. As the music from the boom box faded, music filtering through the blinds on the second story window took its place, and floating across the campus was the musical soundtrack from Franco Zeffirelli's classic production of *Romeo and Juliet*.

Professor Mark Phillips's "Love in Literature" class was nearing its end. The film's credits scrolled up the screen, as most of the females wiped away tears from their faces. If one could get a close-up look at the faces of some of the males in class, they would find quite a few glassy eyes. The clearing of the throats and abundant shifting of various positions in their seats certainly made the statement that the males had been emotionally moved by the motion picture, too. One couple in the back of the class and behind the projector, apparently boyfriend and girlfriend, were holding hands. The girl broke the handhold, wiped her eyes with a tissue, and leaned over and kissed her boyfriend on the cheek. "I'm so glad that we don't have to experience something like that," she whispered in his ear. He looked at her with an approving nod and a caring smile.

Mark addressed his class, "What you have just witnessed, my dear students, is the 'nonpareil' of love." As he looked out over the class, he observed a few raised hands. Having taught the class many times over the years at NGSU, he knew what questions were coming his way. Please look up the word in your Webster's." He gestured toward a student sitting next to the open window, "Mr. Thomas, would you please open the blinds?" The student nodded, and with a slight pull of his hand, the class was filled with early morning sunshine. Mark walked to the front of the class and moved into a lecture mode.

"Ladies and gentlemen, as you are all well aware, we have just completed our next to the last assignment on the subject of love and most, and I say this with a touch of trepidation, most of love's variant nuances. We have covered a great amount of material. We began in Egypt, moved through Greece and Rome, the Middle Ages, Spain, France, and finally ended with Elizabethan England. Sad to say, we have only touched and traversed the first few floors of the skyscraper. Love, as we have discussed previously, is a universal emotion. It is a term that eludes and defies the definitive. However, we have remained somewhat constant down through the ages. What Mr. Ovid had to say to us from ancient Rome can be found on most silver screens and television today." A female student was waving her hand from the third row of desks. "Yes, Miss Burr?"

"Do you think the kind of love between Romeo and Juliet is…What I mean is, is it really real?"

Mark smiled, "If, Miss Burr, you are defining 'real' as existing today, that such a love relationship exists in our present-day society, then I would have to answer in the affirmative. The love experienced by Romeo and Juliet as it existed in the mind of Mr. William Shakespeare is not simply a figment of the imagination."

Another student raised her hand. "Miss Rawlins?"

"Professor Phillips, you've been quite open with us about your first marriage. May I be so bold as to ask you if you have, in your lifetime, ever experienced such an ideal love?" All talking and whispering came to an abrupt halt throughout the class as everyone tuned in to Mark's reply. The class bell rang, but nobody moved. They waited for Mark's answer.

"No, Miss Rawlins, I've not been that fortunate, and at my age, I'm afraid I never will…Class is dismissed!"

Mark returned to the projector to rewind the film as his students filed out for their next class. As the film rewound, Mark thought about his last statement to the class. His memory, took him back to his early twenties when he was a young Marine, home on leave after a tour in Korea. It was then that he met Gloria, the girl that he would marry.

All he could think of was how gorgeous her breasts were. They had to be a size forty. "With tits like that," he'd thought, "I could get the attention of an entire Marine division!" He admitted, with a shake of his head and a slight smile, as he slipped the film back into its case, that in his twenties, his erections overpowered his ability to use his brain. Desire, lust, or just plain old fucking were at the top of his list and at the bottom of Dr. Abraham H. Maslow's. However, Mark thought, "I did need something or someone at that point in time to anchor me down. I was like a ship in a storm. I was drinking too much and was without a purpose in my life. Gloria and my daughters, especially my daughters, slowed me down enough to spearhead my way through three degrees. Without them, I'd never have made it. But love, as experienced between Juliet and Romeo or as expressed by Kahlil Gibran, was never present." Mark closed the door to his classroom and paused a brief moment in the hall, "I truly wonder what that feeling is?"

Dr. George K. Wessel, Chairman of the English Department, hailed the professor from down the hall, "How's it going, Mark? Did you leave them all crying again over Romeo and Juliet?" He caught up with Mark, and both men walked together heading toward their respective offices.

"It never fails." Mark said, "How can you lose with a classic film and the directorial genius of Zeffirelli?"

"I hear that you finally won a game of billiards against Dr. Westmore. Congratulations."

"Thanks. It was a long overdue win."

"I presume that your final lecture for this semester will be supported, as usual, by Mr. Cheddar?"

Mark was surprised. "I thought I told you about Cheddar, George. Mr. Cheddar is now in cheese heaven. He passed away last Christmas."

"Sorry to hear about that." They both stopped outside Dr. Wessel's office.

"A Mr. Limburger has taken his place."

"Love those names." Dr. Wessel thumbed through some mail he'd been carry-ing. "By the way, how is your book progressing?"

"It's creeping up on the halfway mark. This summer..."

Dr. Wessel cut him off. "Sorry to interrupt you, but I just didn't want to for-get to give you this letter. It came to my office by special delivery. It's from Adena Rutherford, Valdosta, Georgia. She just made the scholarship deadline. Anyway, her request falls under your jurisdiction. From what I had time to read, she apparently wants to carry a dual major in English and journalism. Well, got to go." He stepped into his office and stuck his head back out the door, "By the way, your fictional article about Alexander Hamilton that appeared in The New Yorker was excellent, especially as it related to our bicentennial. Good show for 1976. Ohh, and in your last lecture, have fun with Mr, Mr? Ahh..."

"Limburger, George...Mr. Limburger, and thanks for the compliment," Mark said with a nod of his head.

"See you at our final faculty meeting," and with that comment, Dr. Wessel disappeared into his office.

Mark again started moving slowly down the hall towards his office. He removed Adena's letter from the envelope. A photograph dropped to the floor. Mark picked it up and stared at it for a moment. "Another sweet Georgia cracker. Rather plain but has an inner beauty."

*   *   *   *

The Valdosta High School football stadium was decorated to the hilt. Wide silk banners depicting the school colors draped the sides and backs of the stadium bleachers and ran down the aisles of chairs placed on the football field. What once was a field for growing peanuts was now the site for the 1976 graduation ceremonies of Valdosta High. The graduating class of nearly three hundred repre-sented just about every occupation existing in this farm land community. The entire economic base of this area of Georgia rested primarily on farming and the main money-making crops were peanuts, pecans, cotton, and the famous Vidalia onion. Pig farming and wood products from the fast-growing Georgia yellow pine were also at the top of the moneymaking list.

From the farmers and their toil came the industries, government agencies, and private enterprises that supported a farming socio-economic milieu. Most of the parents present at this graduation ceremony were secretly praying that their graduating senior or seniors would be returning to the farm and family. Most of the graduating class had other plans.

Off to the side, in front of the bleachers and almost on the fifty-yard line, was an entire family: grandparents, brothers, sisters, mom and dad, uncles and aunts, and an overabundance of cousins. This clan had their own folding chairs, and it appeared as though they had all been here before. The occasion had become almost a family tradition.

Everyone was dressed in their Sunday best; however, most of the men had all discarded their suit coats and loosened their ties. Kool Aid, iced tea, and perhaps lemonade was being passed around from one family member to the next, and the good old cardboard fans on a stick were getting a workout. The family was well prepared for the high humidity and 80 to 90 degree weather that was normal in South Georgia at this time of year.

A large portable stage had been erected at one end of the field and was fully decorated with school-color buntings. Seated across the back of the stage was the usual high school commencement dignitaries: members of the school board, perhaps a few local politicians looking for votes, faculty, administration, and especially the high school principal. Adena Rutherford was standing at the podium directly in the middle and at the front of the stage. She was nearing the close of her valedictorian address. Her nerves had steadied, but the heat and humidity were beginning to take a toll. Sweat dripped down her face, turning her mascara into puddles of black paint with nowhere to go but down. Even her glasses were beginning to show streams of perspiration.

"…and that brings us to this time and this place, 1976, our nation's bicentennial. Let us move from this period of our lives into an era where there is neither color nor strife. Where all of us, regardless of race…"

Adena's mother squirmed at the mention of race. To soften her reaction to the word and to placate a black couple sitting not too far to her right, she pretended that her physical reaction was simply to reposition her posterior.

"…sex, religion, or age, will be recognized for what we give of ourselves to our home, community, county, state, nation, and planet. I'm sure I speak for all of my graduating classmates when I say that I leave Valdosta High School with more positive than negative memories. And I trust that what I have learned here will serve me as a catalyst to learning the rest of my life."

Adena bowed her head, indicating that her speech had ended, and as she hid her face from the audience and her classmates, tears mixed with her sweat cascaded onto her gown. Her classmates broke into hoots and shouts, whistles, and applause. Four years of high school and their memories, good and bad, just came to an end. Or was this a beginning? The high school band struck up "Pomp and Circumstance," and the graduating class of Valdosta High School, 1976, along with the dignitaries on the stage, started filing out of the stadium. Outside the stadium, pandemonium ruled the moment. Emotions poured forth like mighty waves crashing down on sandy beaches during a storm.

Adena's oldest sister, Delores, was the first one of the family to break through a steady stream of bodies and, like an NFL tackle, she threw her arms around Adena and gave her one of those treasured hugs that is long remembered for its honesty, emotion, and love.

Breaking the hug, Delores stood back and held her sister at arm's length.

"Congratulations, Sis. Your speech was fantastic."

"Thanks, Delores. I can always count on you for a positive stroke. I'm just glad it's over. I was scared to death. Where are the folks?"

"This way." She took Adena by the arm and started escorting her in the direction of the rest of the family.

"This gown makes for a perfect Russian Bath."

"What in the hell is that?" Delores said. "It is a steam box for losing weight. I'll bet I've dropped at least five pounds this afternoon."

"My God!" exclaimed Delores, "Loan it to me!" Both girls started to laugh.

Both girls stooped to avoid getting in the way of a proud graduate picture taking. As they emerged from this potential catastrophe, Adena stopped her sister.

"By the way, how come Sheryl isn't with you?"

"Come on, Adena, you know your younger sister. She got sidetracked by an ex-boyfriend." Delores resumed walking in the direction of the family and suddenly stopped and turned to face her sister.

"Listen, sis, I've got to tell you before we get to the folks how really proud I am of you for giving up the opportunity to study in Spain. I know that it was a tremendous sacrifice on your part, but your decision to attend the clan's Alma Mater made the entire family very happy. I dropped the ball by going to NGSU for only two years and winding up marrying a rich pig farmer. You know Sheryl isn't interested in going to college, period, so you're Mom and Granddaddy's last hope."

As Delores finished her last sentence, their grandfather and grandmother broke through the crowd then hurried toward the girls. "There you are!" they both shouted at once. Delores made one last hasty comment to Adena.

"I love ya, Sis." She and Adena quickly squeezed hands before their grandmother and grandfather embraced Adena. Her grandfather held her at arms length.

"We're so proud of you. And, my, don't we look beautiful in that cap and gown!" Her grandfather turned to look at his wife, "Don't just stand there, Emma. Get a picture of us, and then I'll get a picture of you and Adena. Delores can take a picture of all three of us." As the picture taking ritual evolved, the crowd began to thin out. Standing about twenty feet in front of Adena were her mother and stepfather. They were patiently waiting for Adena to come to them. Everyone acknowledged their presence. Adena gave her grandfather and grandmother another hug and then moved to Delores before going to her parents. Adena quickly whispered in her sister's ear,

"My decision to attend NGSU was made only for our grandfather's benefit." Adena smiled and went to her mother and gave her mother and stepfather a congenial embrace.

"Needless to say, Adena," her mother said, "we are all very proud of you today. Carl and I have made your graduation dinner reservations at the country club, and you know how they are about punctuality."

"Yes, Mother. However, I must turn in my gown and..."

"Carl will pay for your gown, dear." She placed an arm around Adena's shoulder as Carl gestured toward Delores and the grandparents to follow, and they all started walking toward the parking lot.

Adena's mother continued her conversation: "That was an excellent speech, dear. Only I wish I could have read it beforehand. Your comments about the niggers were much too nice." Adena was expecting her mother's comments, so they did not come as a shock. She was prepared with the appropriate response, and with a polite smile said, "I knew they would upset you, Mother, and that is why I didn't let you read it, beforehand."

*   *   *   *

Professor Mark Phillips was standing in front of the class holding a small wire cage containing a white rat. On a portable table, off to his left, was a maze framed by a box. It was Limburger's private apartment. The top of the box was covered with a removable, clear Plexiglas top.

"For the past four months," Mark said, as he moved into his final lecture of the spring semester, "We've been studying, discussing, and analyzing the emotion of love as it has been presented in literature. We stopped with Mr. Shakespeare. Today, to end our semester, and to provide you a little more fodder for the final, we're are going to look at love scientifically. Perhaps the best approach is through the eyes of the Behavioralists. So, we will move in that direction. We can analyze, observe first-hand, and we can deal with the facts and thereby add to our empirical data. I draw your attention to this cage I hold in my hand." Mark held up the cage and began to walk up and down the aisles of the classroom.

"All of you have been introduced to Mr. Limburger. Now I would like to introduce you to Miss Cleopatra. She is in the white box in front of the class. Our new guest just so happens to be in her mating period; consequently, we are going to introduce her to Mr. Limburger's bachelor pad."

Mark went down to the maze and gestured to the class to gather around him. Mr. Limburger, a white rat male, was nestled in the corner of the box gnawing on a large piece of cheddar cheese. The corner of the box containing Mr. Limburger was quite spacious and appeared to be quite cozy. Mr. Limburger finished his cheese, went over to a side wall, pushed a lever, and another chunk of cheese rolled out of a hole in the side of his pad. Satisfied with another sizeable chunk of cheese, he scampered over to another wall and nibbled on a tube that fed him water. Once he had quenched his thirst, he returned to the chunk of cheese.

Mark addressed the class, "As you can see, Mr. Limburger is very much at home. In fact, his home, or should we say, apartment, is probably 70 to 100 percent better than some student apartments located around campus." Several of the students vocalized agreement. "…and, I'm sure, much cleaner." Most of the girls moaned in agreement. "As you can see, our little bachelor is also well fed. All of his physiological needs are met. The maze provides him with an opportunity for exercise and adventure, whenever he chooses to avail himself. We're now going to add a little variation to his usual, everyday lifestyle."

Mark removed Cleopatra from her box and placed her in a room opposite Limburger's. They had to find one another. As soon as Cleopatra was placed in the maze, both rats moved toward one another. Limburger forgot his hunk of cheese. Before they could meet in the maze, Mark drew a curtain across the top of the box. A groan of disappointment came from the audience, along with a few chuckles, and giggles from the female students.

"Now, now," Mark said. "All of God's creatures have a right to privacy, even rats. My first question to this debauched audience is, will or can, Mr. Limburger fall in love?" All of the students raised their hands; some were waving them frantically in an attempt to be the first one called upon. Mark pointed to Ms. Sullivan, who was standing close to the maze.

"Yes, Ms. Sullivan?"

"Professor, I hate to say it, but what is going on in this box is pure sex." Laughter and general commotion exploded from the students.

"Okay, students." yelled Mark, "Put a lid on it." He pointed to another student, "Mr. Taylor?"

"What Mr. Limburger is doing is dictated by animal instinct. No emotion is present. Love, and this is my belief, is non-existent as a concept among the lower animals."

"Very good observation, Mr. Taylor. Very good indeed."

Mark peeked under the curtain covering the maze and then opened it. Limburger was back in his corner, and Cleopatra was roaming around the maze. Mark lifted the Plexiglass top and returned Cleopatra to her box. He rested her box on top of the maze and gestured for the students to return to their desks. He continued his lecture.

"According to the Behavioralists, love is basically the same thing for all animals, that includes homo sapiens. Love, they claim, is a feeling—a good feeling. Whenever an animal feels *good* about something, whether it be the environment, another animal or even an object, it is in love. Mr. Limburger loves his corner and his box. Over a long experiment, even with Cleo present, Limburger could come to love his corner more than Cleo. He might love his corner so much that, if we took it away from him, we might witness a scene similar to Romeo's last scene in Shakespeare's *Romeo and Juliet.*" Once again, the students eagerly started waving their hands and signaling an eagerness for open discussion.

*   *   *   *

Hanover Hall, or Hitler's Haven, as it was popularly called by the female students that occupied it, was quiet that night as the students prepared for final examinations. Miss Carol Sullivan was in her room, sitting at her desk, going over her notes from Professor Phillips' class. Her roommate, Judy Hanover, entered the room, tossed her library books onto her desk and fell backward onto her disarrayed bunk. Looking blankly at the ceiling, she asked Carol, "Are you still studying for your *love* final? Or are you getting wet pants dreaming about Professor Phillips?"

Carol chuckled, "Both."

Judy sat up, "He can certainly make that course interesting."

Carol sighed, "Yeah, he sure can, and when you sit for an hour and look at someone whose face looks like Robert Redford's and who has a body like Sly Stallone's, the course becomes super interesting."

Judy laughed and fell back on her bunk, "I think you might be stretching the Stallone bit."

"Well, maybe a little. But he's close."

Carol jumped up from her chair and crossed to Judy's bunk. "Say, Judy? Is it true that Professor Phillips is dating a Phi Mu?"

"It's true, and the crazy thing is, she isn't even a senior."

"Wow!"

Judy got up from her bed and started to get undressed. "Don't get any ideas, Miss Freshie. He dates students on occasion but never anyone younger than juniors. Below the junior level lies Jail Bait Heaven."

"Do you have any idea how old he is?" Carol asked.

"No, but the general consensus places him in his late forties."

"He looks a lot younger. Do you have any more information about our professor that comes from 'consensus'?"

Judy got into her bathrobe and threw a towel around her neck. "Can you wait until I take my shower?"

"No!"

Judy returned to her bunk and motioned her roommate to sit. "All I know is what kind of common gossip has been passed from student to student. He apparently went through a wicked divorce about two or three years ago. His wife was supposedly having affairs with anything or anybody that carried a good, stiff dick."

Carol got excited and moved closer to Judy, "No kidding?! Go on."

"Anyway, he spent a year after the divorce trying to get custody of his youngest daughter. His two oldest daughters, were of legal age and opted to live with him. After losing his bid for his youngest, and almost losing everything he owned, he started dating and has been going strong ever since."

"Damn, why couldn't I be a junior!"

Judy jumped up from the bunk and headed toward the hallway. As she crossed, she tossed her exit lines over her shoulder, "You might be a junior some day, but for right now, there are two real important things you gotta do."

"Yes? And those are?"

"Pass your upcoming exams and change your wet underpants." With that remark, Judy quickly left the room laughing. Carol threw a note pad at her as she disappeared out the door.

CHAPTER 3

▼

"If you wished to be loved, love."

—Seneca

What purpose does spring serve except to usher in birth or celebrate a new beginning? What is that mystical smell that permeates the air of late spring when the night air is crisp, and a warmth blankets the daylight hours? What is that music that seems to float in the early evening mist, celebrating all the past realities as they merge into everlasting memories? What magic moment engulfs us when we rejoice in a moment of triumph and yet know deep in our hearts that we are stepping across a new threshold of life? As we sing and laugh, drink and dance, we are totally aware that we are participating in a ritual not only of gladness but also of sadness, of things that we have accomplished and of things that we will be leaving behind.

The academic year of 1975–76 at NGSU had ended. For the seniors, it was a time to party and say goodbye; for the majority of students, it was a moment of jubilation for simply moving on to the next year. The evening air was chilly. The smell of honeysuckle mixed with the distinct aroma of pot filtered through the loosely screened windows of a student's off-campus abode. A hastily painted sign hung over the front porch entrance declaiming, "English—Drama—Journalism Party!" Below the exclamation was, "Goodbye Seniors and Good Luck." Rock music, mixed with the sound of laughter and the clinking of glasses, came from within. A few students were talking and milling around outside, and a handful were on the porch passing around a joint. A celebration was in progress. A few of the younger faculty were inside the ramshackle apartment enjoying the revelry along with their students. Some of the students were dancing; others, in the shadowed corners, were making out. The booze, ice, mixers, and finger food, if it could be called food, was laid out in various locations in the kitchen. Needless to say, the kitchen was the most popular room in the house, besides the one bathroom. Professor Mark Phillips was standing by the kitchen sink with one hand holding a scotch and the other caressing the waist of Susan Wells, the embodiment of the typical sorority girl. Inside her attractive head, covered with an impeccable blonde coiffure, was intelligence, an attribute she displayed sparingly. According to Susan, her one and only negative aspect was her height. She felt that being short put her at a disadvantage in life because short women, in her estimation, regardless of the endeavor or situation, always came out at the end of the line. However, for this moment in time, she was content and the envy of every female student at NGSU. She was dating none other than the Professor Mark Phillips. She and Mark were both laughing at an off color joke.

Mark's middle daughter, Salina, was moving through the crowd gathered around her dad (mostly females). Such adoration was something Salina had grown accustomed to since her dad and mother divorced. Her father, in one swipe of an attorney's pen, became the most eligible bachelor in the entire county.

Salina's height of only five foot four inches, along with her attempt to balance three full drinks, made her journey through the crowd a bit slow and awkward. Salina's muscular, athletic build helped bump a few stubborn individuals out of the way, including a few attractive males. Her 'jock' physical appearance did not hinder her in any way because her feminine statistics accentuated the positive: a small waist, a well developed bosom, and her heart-shaped derriere was the envy of most of her high school friends, as well as a major portion of the female students at NGSU. Her brown eyes appeared to be a blend of chocolate and dark, roasted Columbian coffee beans. Her smile and laugh were contagious, and her presence in any group always added excitement to the occasion. She emanated a "Salina Only" bravura, and she was always the life of the party. To know her for a short moment created a feeling of knowing her for an eternity. Her brown hair was thick; a feature inherited from her father. Its thickness only lent itself to enhancing her pixie-style haircut, a hair style that complemented her frolicking nature. She would be graduating Friday, not from the college but from high school. This party was also her celebration. On this particular evening, she wanted to embrace the world, but for the moment, Magnolia, Georgia, would have to suffice. The world was waiting just around the corner.

Salina finally made it through the front lines and reached out her hand to the center of attention.

"Here you are, Dad. I had the feeling that by the time I returned, your glass would be empty, and how right I was." As she handed Mark his scotch and soda, she turned to Susan, "Are you sure I can't get you anything, Susan?"

"I'm fine, I've been nursing this drink since I arrived." She glanced at the drinks being held by Salina. "Are you catching up for lost time, or do you usually indulge in two at a time?"

Mark said, "You have aroused my curiosity along with Susan's. Are you catching up?"

Salina laughed, "No, folks, one is for me, and the other is for the love of my life, who just arrived."

"I thought he had to work overtime at the barn this evening," Mark said.

"His dad felt sorry for him."

And with that remark, Salina disappeared out the back door of the kitchen. The screen door slammed behind her, jarring loose a little more of the screen mesh that supposedly protected the humans within from the onslaught of spring mosquitoes.

The reverberating sound of the slamming screen door was replaced by Barry Manilow's "I Write The Song." The music was coming from the front room, the nights official dance area for this evening's party. Mark moved his lips close to Susan's ear and whispered, "Listen. Finally a slow song. Let's dance." He took her hand and led her toward the front room. As he left the kitchen area, he graciously bid the kitchen crowd adieu and turned his utmost attention to Susan.

"Have I told you how beautiful you look this evening?"

"A thousand times." She stood up on her toes and kissed him on the lips, "But do me a favor and don't stop."

"How does it feel to finally be a senior?" Mark put his arm around Susan's waist and pulled her close to him. He moved his left arm back behind his waist, and they began to dance. Their bodies could not have been any closer unless they were naked.

"It feels great. I've been waiting for this next year for a long time. How does Salina feel about finishing high school? Doesn't she graduate next Friday?"

"She's elated about finishing high school. And, before you ask I will tell you that, at the moment, she has no intentions of attending college. I'm disappointed, but...And, yes, to answer your question, she graduates next Friday."

Susan started to ask another question, and Mark gently released her hand and put his finger lightly across her lips. "You exit from my life tomorrow for three months. Just breathe heavily into my ear and melt that beautiful body into mine."

Manilow came to an end and was replaced by Donna Summer's "Love To Love You, Baby." Mark leaned his head back, "Ohh, no." Susan answered his cry with, "What do you mean, 'Ohh, no?' You know damn well that you can out-dance anyone here. Let's do it to it."

The dance floor became crowded as bodies identified with the music and began to undulate and bounce up and down, as each person did their own thing. Halfway through the music, Mark grabbed Susan by the hand and headed for the front door. For Mark and Susan a celebration had ended, and an evening of ecstasy was soon to begin.

The next morning, a tired Mark Phillips, said goodbye to Susan as she left Magnolia and headed for the big city of Atlanta. Mark went over to his car and thought to himself, "Fall is a long way off, and I feel lonely already." He smiled and hopped in his car to take advantage of a new self-serve Tenneco filling station just opening in town. He didn't want to pass up regular gas at thirty-eight cents a gallon.

When Mark finished fueling up his car, he glanced at the cashier's window, and to his surprise, Regina, his oldest daughter, was the cashier. He knew immediately that he had made a wrong decision to gas up early in the morning. He hadn't seen Regina in nearly a month, and they hadn't talked to one another in over six months. The last time Mark accidentally crossed Regina's path was at the local Winn-Dixie grocery store. They didn't say a word to one another, but Mark spotted a large black and blue mark on her right cheek. It took every ounce of restraint he could muster to keep from going over to his daughter's apartment and blowing the head off her boyfriend, or even better yet, loading his crotch up with twelve gauge shot so that his fucking days would be over.

Mark walked to the cashier's window with his money already in his hand. Regina recognized her dad's car as soon as it pulled into the station. She wanted to leave, to disappear, but she was the only attendant on duty. As Mark placed his money at the opening of the window, he took a quick glance at his daughter's face. She didn't make eye contact. Once again, he saw a bruised face. A large bruise was visible on one side of her face, and one of her eyes was bloodshot and swollen. He opened his mouth to say something to her, but nothing came out. His eyes were getting blurry, and his anger was about to erupt. He made a brusque exit from the cashier's window and left the new filling station with two tire marks, each one about four feet in length. After her father's hasty and enraged departure, Regina broke down and began to cry.

Two days passed, and Mark was still seething; however, he found some solace in returning to his manuscript. It was early evening, and Mark was trying to concentrate on composition. To help him concentrate and to calm down his still-boiling temper, his favorite Rachmaninoff music was playing in the background. Salina entered the front room and paused in the doorway leading to her bedroom.

"Did you forget? This evening is supposed to be my night out. One of my graduation presents. Remember?" She moved to her dad and put her arms around his neck.

"Just one more sentence. Got to complete my thought."

"You're hitting those keys awfully hard. Which means only one thing." She went around to the side of his chair, "That you're very upset with me or just angry in general. You get to know a person when you have lived with them." She gestured around the small garage apartment, "…in close quarters for three or four years."

Mark stopped typing, stared at his typewriter for a quick moment, and then blurted out, "It's that son-of-a-bitch animal your sister is in love with!"

"Ohh, ohh. You ran into Regina again."

"Yes, and once again she carries some fist-applied tattoos on her face!" Mark spun around in his chair and looked into the eyes of Salina. "What in the hell is the matter with her, Salina? Why is she defying all sense of reason? I just…" He was about to lose control of his emotions ""I just can't understand why."

Salina dropped down on her knees and lifted her father's face. His eyes were moist.

"Dad, you're writing a book about love, and you tell me that you don't understand. I promise you, somewhere along the line you will discover the answer to your own question." She gently touched his face with one of her hands, "And now I need to ask you a favor. This night is supposed to belong to me. It'll be the last full evening that you and I will be able to share for awhile. Can we put off talking about my sister until another time? I love her, and I love you, but…"

Mark adjusted his chair and moved his arms up through Salina's and placed his hands on her face. "Forgive me sweetheart. I apologize." He quickly pulled himself together, and with a melodramatic flair said, "What is it to be, my little chickadee?! Pizza, steak, chicken, gourmet hambur-gar? The fast food establishments in this great city are at your beck and call. Or, if you prefer, we could go to the Holiday Inn and be treated to a decent meal." He crossed his fingers behind his back "And, if you use your imagination, you might perceive a touch of European epicureanism sprinkled with a dash of manners."

Salina jumped up, "Pizza sounds great!"

"Why is my benevolence never rewarded?" asked Mark in a rather subdued tone.

They laughed, put their arms around one another, and headed for the local pizza parlor.

Rachmaninoff was replaced by Elton John, Rod Stewart, and K. C. and the Sunshine Band. The juke box was going non-stop and the smell of oregano, cheese, and baking pizza dough filled the restaurant. Mark and Salina were in conversation, waiting for their pizza.

"Do I have your blessing?"

"You know you do, Salina. You and Barry haven't talked about anything else this past year. I trust that you'll keep your promise to me and keep in touch. Not only are you two taking on a challenge but one helluva adventure."

"Not to worry, Dad. You will be contacted every time we make port."

The waitress delivered their 'large everything on it' pizza. Space was cleared, and slices were selected. The conversation continued with Mark's comment.

"There must be a great deal of money in tobacco."

"It also helps to be the only son, and when you are, graduation awards can be on the Neiman Marcus level."

"Still, a sixty-foot sailboat is not your average college graduation present!"

"And my sweetheart can't wait to sail it. You know, he's been sailing since he was ten years old. His cousin, Dwight, has been sailing for the last 30 years. I'd say that he is an expert in the sport. His wife will also be giving us an experienced hand."

"I have no worries about Barry's sailing expertise. Are you forgetting that I have sailed with you on the lake, at least twice; however, I am relieved that you'll have two very experienced companions going along on this adventure."

Salina shook hot pepper flakes onto her slice of pizza and continued the conversation with one of her pixie smiles.

"How about some real pepper-upper news?"

"Shake it on me. I'm ready for anything. I think."

"When Barry and I get back from our world sail?"

"Yes?"

"Well, I've decided to send my brains to college. It's all wrapped up in our future wedding plans. Barry wants me to be his educational equal. Besides, I can attend NGSU for nothing. So why not?" She saw the elation move across her father's face.

Mark's smile went from ear to ear. "Thanks for the graduation present, and I'm not even graduating. That is the best news I've heard in a long, long time. Now that you've made my day...Where will you, Barry, and the others be departing from?"

Salina wrapped some dangling mozzarella cheese around her finger and guided it to where it belonged and then answered Mark's question.

"Miami. From there, we plan to lolly around the Caribbean for awhile, take in South America, and when the typhoon season ends in the Pacific, were off to Australia and then the Orient."

Mark shook his head and began to laugh, "Mind if I tag along?" Salina joined in his laughter, stood, and grabbed him by the arm.

"Come on. Time to exercise off some of this pizza. I know you'll hate this, but are you ready for our special night at the local college bistro? Keep in mind that half of the college crowd has split town, so it won't be too crowded."

"What have I done to deserve such glorious torture? Mark offered his arm. Lead on, Lady McTeen. It's on to the Purple Passion." With a flair, they exited the pizza parlor.

*   *   *   *

Salina was partially correct. The parking lot of the Purple Passion was only 3/4's full instead of overflowing. College and high school students were lingering around outside. Vehicle traffic was in a constant state of flux. Cars and trucks were moving in and out of the parking lot and moving from one parking space to another. A large purple neon sign lit up the front of the club proclaiming that this was the infamous Purple Passion beer joint.

Back in the early forties and through the fifties, the huge barn that became the "Passion Hut" was once the most popular honky-tonk nightclub of Magnolia. Country and western music reigned and legend had it that Hank Williams sang his first song there. After the fifties and the birth of rock and roll, the music shaking the walls of the Passion changed to hard rock and heavy metal; however, the flow of beer remained about the same. If one desired something more alcoholic than beer, they had to find it under the stars. In their off season, NGSU athletes served as law enforcers at the club and kept things, for the most part, on an even keel. The Passion, the only 'hot' college nightclub in Magnolia, was usually a safe place to let out emotions and to toss all cares to the wind on certain occasions. This particular evening, with the spring semester coming to a close, was one of those certain occasions.

Music from a live band, imported from Atlanta for the special occasion, was blaring, and the old wooden walls of the Passion were allowing the sound to freely pass through the boards to flood the nighttime air. As Salina and Mark approached the entrance, they were met with a continuous line of proven twenty-one-and-over individuals exiting the club with their hands loaded with large Dixie cups filled with beer for their friends and compatriots outside who were not old enough to go inside.

Mark took Salina's arm. "Are you sure this is where you want to go? It's going to take us forever to get in." Salina whispered quickly in his ear, "Don't worry about it, dad. My friend is on the door tonight." A young man standing about six feet seven inches and weighing about two hundred and eighty pounds called her to the front of the line and gave her a big hug. As he held Salina above the ground, he turned and looked at Mark. "She gets in free, sir, but I'm afraid that I will have to charge you the two-dollar cover charge." Salina quickly whispered in the young man's ear. Mark reached for his wallet and withdrew two bucks. The young man told him that he could put his money back in his wallet and then stamped his hand with a small icon that resembled some kind of withered passion fruit.

Mark, led by Salina, made their way through the crowd to the bar. Salina pulled out some crushed bills from her Levi pocket, and Mark gestured for her to put them away. The drinks were on him. They spotted a couple vacating a table on the opposite side of the dance floor and started maneuvering toward it.

As they moved across the dance floor, they attempted a conversation, but the noise of the crowd, coupled with the noise of the band, was over-powering their words, even when they attempted dialogue at full volume. They finally navigated to the free table near a party of six college boys. None of them recognized Professor Phillips, but one of the boys recognized Salina. It appeared that none of them was in a normal state of being. Apparently, they had been partying for some time. The young man who recognized Salina was making a slightly shaky cross toward her table and waving to her in an attempt to capture her attention, which he did. Salina took a large gulp of beer and then grabbed her dad by the arm. "Come on, Dad! Let's dance."

"Already?!...I haven't..."

"A creep is heading this way. Wesley Snipes, I've met him before, and believe me, he is an A—number—one Georgia Cracker and a drunk one. Rescue me, dear knight!" She took her father's hand and pulled him to the dance floor.

One of the six boys sitting at the nearby table, who resembled a young Charles Atlas (a definite body-builder), gave Wesley a rap on the head when he returned to the group. "Looks like you ain't gonna get a dance with that good looking ass, Wes. They got out on that dance floor, and it looks to me like they plan on staying out there for a good while. I swear, the way she moves that ass has given me a hard." Another member of the group threw a question at Wesley.

"Say, Wes? Ain't that the professor whose daughter is…"

"That's him all right."

The body-builder said, "Yeah, I know who ya'll are talking about. Is that his daughter? You know, the one we were talking about?"

Wesley replied, "Yeah, that's his daughter, but not the one you all are talking about."

The body-builder came on again, "Hey, guys, I got an idea. We can have a little fun when they get back to their table." He motioned his friends to gather around and loudly voiced his plans.

Mark crossed back toward the table and two lonely, warm beers. Salina remained on the dance floor with a friend. Mark sat and hesitantly took a sip of his warm brew. Meanwhile, the body-builder was making an unsteady approach toward Mark's table. He stopped midway and shouted out at a level where the entire club could hear, "Say, Professor? Ain't you the professor who's daughter is living with a big, black nigger?"

The body-builder turned around to his buddies with a smile, and they in turn gave him their thumbs-up support.

Mark looked at his tormentor, "I beg your pardon?" was the only reply Mark could muster.

The muscle-man turned back to face Mark and took another couple of steps forward. Once again he shouted out with a laugh, "Begging who, Professor? I said, ain't you the prof with a daughter living with a nigger?"

Salina had broken loose from her dance partner and was racing across the dance floor toward her father. The rock group on stage had stopped playing. Mark knew that possible hell could break loose. Any altercation in the club could get him into trouble with the university administration, and he wasn't sure of what was going to happen to Salina when he saw her moving in his direction across the dance floor.

His mind snapped into an immediate plan of action. He stood up and took the necessary steps toward the muscle-man and held out his hand, and with a boisterous voice exclaimed, "Young man, it's my pleasure to meet you!"

He shook the boy's hand vigorously. "For years I've looked forward—for years, mind you—to meeting an individual whose cerebrum and cerebellum were left on his sire's testicle, thereby bungling the process of a decent conception. You, sir, are an anomaly of the highest order. Good night, sir." He broke the handshake and reached for Salina's hand. Both turned and headed straight toward the front door as quickly as their legs could carry them. The body-builder stood dumbfounded. He didn't know exactly what had been said to him, but he knew the professor's words had tromped him in front of his peers. He heard laughter coming from the students that had surrounded the scene expecting a brawl. Wesley moved to the body-builder and quickly explained what the professor had said to him. Rage filled the muscle-man, he bellowed, and at the same time, shoved everyone aside that was in his way as he bolted after Mark.

Salina had managed to get into Mark's car, and Mark had time to open the driver's side door when a big hand clamped down on his shoulder and spun him around. He stood face to face with the body-builder. The first thing that popped into his mind was that they were outside, making this excuse for a human being fair game.

"My buddies told me, in plain English, what you said to me, Mr. Professor. So, I decided to get a piece of your ass."

Mr. Atlas hauled back his right arm and prepared to strike a blow to Mark's left cheek. Salina saw the movement before her Dad and yelled, "Watch out for his right, Dad!" Mark countered with two movements as a crowd from inside the club gathered for the show. Mark stopped Mr. Atlas's swing in mid-air and made a mighty right-hand blow into the body-builder's solar plexus. The impact of the blow ushered forth a loud groan and grunt from Mark's opponent. Mark followed the abdomen punch with a swift, powerful, left upper-cut, and the body-builder was out for the night.

Mark got in the car with a stunned Salina. "I detest violence, but I thank God, especially at this moment, for my boxing years in the Marines!" He turned to look at his daughter as he turned on the ignition, and with a smile said, "I trust you had an exciting evening? Happy graduation, sweetheart." His foot found the accelerator, and they departed the Purple Passion parking lot.

*   *   *   *

Early morning, a week after the night at the Purple Passion, just below Mark's Bohemian garage apartment, Barry Bremmer, Salina's boyfriend, was loading the last piece of her luggage into his car. Salina stood at the edge of the driveway with her father. She was finding her final words to her father very difficult to utter. Each voiced goodbye became more emotional.

"Once again, goodbye, Dad. And again, I'm sorry about what happened last week."

"Hey, forget it. I haven't experienced something like that in many, many years." Mark began to laugh, "In fact, for just a few moments, I felt like a young man. However, the morning after when I crawled out of bed, my body told me otherwise."

Salina finally worked up the courage to turn and face her father for the final goodbye. She reached out her arms and embraced his neck.

"Good luck with the book, and give my love to Theresa when she comes to visit this summer. It's going to be a strange summer without her in it. Tell her that I'll come to Texas to see her when Barry and I get back to the States." She paused, not for words but for the emotion that was building up in her body. "And please, when you see Regina, give her my love." She pulled herself close to her dad and put her head against his shoulder "And, most of all, I love you, Dad. Thanks for all your love and trust that you've given me through the years…and also for your faith in me." She kissed him gently on the cheek and broke her embrace.

Mark took her by the hands. His voice was about to crack, "Everything given has been repaid with happiness." Mark slowly dropped her hands with a strange feeling that somehow he wanted to hold her forever. He walked over to Barry. "Barry, I'm entrusting my daughter into your care." He reached out to shake hands but instead embraced him. "Take care of my little girl and love her, and for God's sake, both of you come back to me."

Mark broke the embrace, and Barry grabbed his hand, "I'll watch over her with my life, Mr. Phillips. I love her as much as you do."

"I can't ask for anything more,"

Barry and Salina got into the car. The doors closed, and Mark crossed to Salina's open window. Mark bent down and, with all of the emotional control he could muster, gave Salina one last kiss.

"Okay, you two, get the hell out of here quick before you see this old man break down."

Barry started the car and backed out of the driveway. Mark saw their waves thru blurred vision as his tears moved down and covered his face. Those sounds that come from the heart and the soul in the most emotional hours came pouring forth: His last daughter had been taken from him by the currents of life. As he walked back, alone, to his apartment, all he could hear in his mind's ear was the laughter of his three little daughters, and all he could see were the three of them sitting on his lap as he read to them, with a little paraphrasing, Longfellow's poem, *The Children's Hour.*

"…From my study I see in the lamplight,
Descending the broad hall stair,
Grave Regina and laughing Salina,
And Theresa with golden hair…"

CHAPTER 4

▼

"Sometimes we are less unhappy in being deceived by those we love,
than in being undeceived by them."

—Francois Duc De La Rochefoucauld

Laughter rang out among the trees and shadows somewhere between the borders of Georgia and Tennessee. The smell of jasmine permeated the air, and the dogwoods, the trees of the crucified Christ, according to legend, were in full bloom, helping to hide from probing eyes two youths astride two powerful horses in full gallop. The moving silhouettes of horse and rider against the panorama of white dogwood blossoms created a picture that might be plucked right from Shakespeare's *A Mid-Summer Night's Dream*. The young riders could have cared less about where they were in the world, for youth and love recognize no boundaries, and for a brief time in their world of reality, time seemed to stand still just for them.

The magnificent black stallion was the first to break into a clearing. His rider led him toward a huge, tall Georgia Yellow Pine. Its size intimidated all of the other trees in the surrounding area. The rider dismounted, walked to the base of the tree, and shouted out into the silence of the forest, "I've found our tree!" A heart that had been carved in the massive tree was facing him. Inside the heart were the carvings, G. M. + A. R.. A date, 1974, was carved just below the heart. The young rider ran his hand through his long, black hair in a quick attempt at improving his appearance. His ruddy complexion matched the exposed red clay earth beneath his feet. He was rather tall and lanky, and his earthy, deep, dark brown eyes had dilated a bit upon the discovery of the carvings in the tree. He ran his fingers gently across them as the second rider entered the clearing. Adena quickly dismounted, "You tricked me on that last turn, or I would have been here first." Gary turned to the disheveled Adena and with a short laugh replied, "You're just not in top form today, Adena. Look! He pointed to the carving, "There it is, I told you we'd find it."

Adena walked to the foot of the tree and into the shade. She made a quick attempt at tucking her hair back into its bun arrangement, and collapsed onto the ground, stretched out her body, and looked up into the myriad clusters of pine needles. Each one appeared to point to the heavens.

"It seems like so long ago since we made our mark on that tree," she sighed. Gary sat down beside her. Still looking up at the carving, he said, "Only two years ago, but it feels like ten." He shook his head in disbelief and looked at Adena, "So many changes. Time seems to move by faster in your late teens. Do you think the days will move faster for us in our twenties?"

Adena's attention moved from the tree to Gary's eyes. "Are you ready for this fall?" questioned Adena.

"I'm not sure."

"Don't you still want to be a mortician?"

"The money potential still interests me. I'd never be at a loss for clientele." They both worked up a laugh as he continued, "How is your summer job going at the newspaper?"

"Great. The editor asked me to write a couple of features. My first assignment will be about our beloved Vidalia onion."

Gary laughed, "The Vidalia onion?!" Adena put on a serious face, "That subject area, sir, is not a laughing matter." Sniffing and pretending to wipe tears from her eyes, she joined Gary in his laughter.

Their laughter faded when their eyes met. Gary moved his face ever so slowly toward Adena's and wrapped one of his arms around her. Their lips touched and lingered upon each other, and their breathing began to move from normal to hot.

There was a quivering of their flesh as they both moved backwards and became part of the earth. Their hearts were beating to a rhythm of passion, a passion that knew life and was as much a part of life as the tree that served as their umbrella from the sun. As they moved from the controlled to the uncontrolled, Gary moved his hand over Adena's breast, and for a moment began to apply a soft, sensual massage. Adena slowly removed his hand, braced herself, and moved upward to a sitting position, forcing Gary to do likewise.

"I'm not ready for this, Gary," said Adena in a breathy voice.

"You were ready two years ago. Remember? Only we were interrupted by a couple of hunters who entered our world at the wrong time."

"Dear, Gary."

As she spoke, she reached up and touched his face, "I've changed during the past two years, and so have you. Perhaps we have grown a bit wiser since our last visit to this place and to this tree."

"But…"

"I don't love you, Gary, and what we almost did two years ago and what we were moving toward today should be some kind of love's extension. I can't explain any more than that." Adena saw the hurt expressed on Gary's face as he turned away from her.

"What is love, Adena?" How do you recognize it? I know, somehow, that I love you. My mind and my body tell me so…but…"

Adena rested her head against his shoulder. "I don't know what love is. All I know is that it takes two to complete the circle, and our circle isn't complete. Believe me, Gary, my body wanted you. It screamed out to me, but my mind said no. I'm sorry, Gary, and I ask you to forgive me for leading you on. I'm asking you to be my friend."

Gary, with bowed head and misty eyes, replied in a whisper that only Adena and the old Georgia Yellow Pine could have heard, a whisper hidden from the world that came from the heart of a young boy, "I will be your friend, Adena. A friend that will love you forever."

*   *   *   *

The tables were covered with burgundy tablecloths, accented with emerald green cloth napkins. The stainless steel eating utensils were in their proper place. Each table was decorated with a vase of varied flowers and by a deep red crystal vessel, each containing a votive candle. The carpet was printed with a dusty pastel, rose pattern that complemented what appeared to be green damask wallpaper. For Magnolia, Georgia, the local Holiday Inn put on quite a show. It was the only restaurant in town with a touch of metropolitan class; consequently, it catered to the town's elite and to parents visiting the town or the university. The rooms were spacious and clean, the pool was extra large, and the patio was an excellent location for special outdoor parties and elaborate festivities. The Irish Pub or bar was the best in town and hired only the most professional bartenders available.

Located not too far from the bar was one of the most polished Steinway Grand Pianos in all of East Georgia. Through the years, it had provided many employment opportunities to many young, talented music majors from the university. According to rumor, Rachmaninoff, Van Cliburn, and Roger Williams had played the old grand when they made their appearances at NGSU and had to spend an evening at the Inn.

Mark Phillips was sitting close to the grand piano. The afternoon was quickly fading, and Mark's scotch and soda glass was getting empty. Dr. Westmore was up at the bar finishing up a long telephone call from his office. He hung up the phone and walked back toward the table where Mark was downing his last drop of scotch. Will turned quickly back to the bar and shouted to Casey the bartender.

"My God, Casey! Bring our Professor Phillips a refill before he keels over and I have to administer CPR!" Will continued to the table, and Casey mixed up a quick scotch and soda. "Sorry I took so long, but the call was from my office. Mrs. Wilkins is in the first stages of labor, which means I'll be on my way to the hospital within the next hour to make another fast delivery." Will shook his head, "This will be her twelfth kid. Anyway, where were we before the phone interruption?" He sat at the table as Casey delivered Mark's drink. Mark exchanged glasses and thanked Casey for the fast delivery.

Casey started back toward the bar with a question, "How about you, Dr. Westmore? Another beer?"

"Can't afford another one, Casey. I have to be leaving for the hospital in short order. But thanks."

"Say, Will?" asked Mark, "That Mrs. Wilkins? Wasn't she the one that almost pulled you out of the opening night of *Macbeth?*" Mark, recapturing the incident from the past, started to laugh.

"She's the one." replied Will, "By the way Mark, when are you going to direct another Shakespeare for the drama department? You know how much damn enjoyment I had playing the part of Macduff. I especially relished that final scene when I entered carrying the head of that no good son-of-a-bitch, Macbeth!"

Mark turned to look Will in the eyes. "And do you know how many heart failures you gave me during rehearsals when you had to rush off to the hospital?!" Mark once again began to laugh, "Every time the phone rang backstage during the performances, I cringed. But…the show made it, and you gave one hell of a performance!"

"Memories, memories." Will shifted in his seat and rested his elbow and forearm on the table, "I do believe, before the phone interruption, that you were telling me something about you and your ex-wife."

Mark took a swallow of his scotch, "Well, you now know how we met. I wish our departure was as colorful and as interesting. However, you have some idea of what a young, horny, uneducated U.S. Marine can do when his brain is located in his pelvic area. I still contend that one could see my wife approach a corner before her torso came into view." Will smiled and slowly shook his head. Mark continued, "I've got to tell you, Will, that when Gloria was young, she was a knockout. When I was at Boston University, I took her to a BU and Army football game. She was about three months pregnant with Salina at the time, but she didn't show at all. Anyway, her boobs had inflated to about a double D cup size. She wore a sweater to the game, and when we walked into the stadium, every cadet present gasped and eyed her like they were trying to gauge the exact distance for a personal rocket launch."

Will had received a phone call from Mark early that morning asking him if he had the time to join him for lunch at the Holiday Inn. Will had learned over the years that whenever Mark called and asked for a lunch date, he had something on his mind to either let go or to celebrate. For the past year, most of their lunches gave Mark an opportunity to vent his emotions over his divorce from Gloria. Will would simply pass on lunch and sit with a glass of tea or coffee, and sometimes a beer, as Mark unloaded to a friend.

"Mark, I've never asked you this particular question before, and if you don't want to answer it, I can understand, but what really happened between you and Gloria to bring about such an abrupt split?"

Mark shifted in his seat and sat silent for a few moments. Taking another sip from his glass, he answered Will's question, "She went one way with her life, and I went another. She decided that a high school education was all she needed, and I decided that I wanted to go as high as I could go. We also changed sexually. A year before coming to Magnolia she began to change. She wanted sex every day of the week and two or three times a day." He paused, "I couldn't figure it out, Will, and to this day, I can't understand her change in behavior. Maybe it was because her youth was ebbing away, or maybe she was having some kind of reaction to early menopause. In the final analysis, my sexual drive that had once kept both of us busy and satisfied no longer fit the bill; consequently, she was finding her outlet with anyone in the county who was looking for a one-night, morning, or afternoon stand. I still had a powerful sex drive and still do; however, when you're married to a nympho, enough is never enough, if that makes sense. I'm surprised you didn't hear about it somewhere along the way. She was not a disciple of discretion."

Will called out to Casey who was busy preparing the bar for the evening trade. "Hey, Casey?"

"Yes, Dr. Westmore?" came from behind the bar.

"When you get the chance, bring me a tall glass of iced tea. Thanks." Will turned back to Mark, "Sorry about how it all ended. Now I know why you all separated. It was tough for me to understand because I thought you two made the ideal couple from the very first day you all walked into my office." Casey delivered the glass of iced tea and returned to the bar.

Mark finished the last of his scotch and soda as Will tried to lighten up the somber mood. "What do you say we talk about something a little lighter. Like, where is Salina? You know that your girls are almost like my own daughters."

"I was going to tell you about her when you returned to the table, but I got a little side tracked. She and Barry Bremmer are somewhere in Barbados."

"Damn, what I wouldn't give for an experience like that. Maybe, just maybe, I can plan a trip like that for my wife and me, once the kids are out of college.... And, Regina? How is she doing? I haven't seen her in...damn...almost a year! She used to stop by my office at least once a month just to say hello." Casey returned from the bar with another drink for Mark and quickly swapped the empty for the full, smiled, and headed back to the bar. Mark watched him make the swap, and before he could say, "Thank you," Casey was gone. Mark just shook his head and said, "Damn, he's good."

Will continued, "And, you haven't brought her into any of our recent lunch conversations. What's going on?" Will looked into Mark's eyes and saw them begin to mist up. Will knew right away that he had just touched on the real reason for today's lunch meeting.

Mark's eyes dropped from Will down toward the table. His speech descended into what sounded like a deep cavern and was barely audible, "Haven't you heard about the NGSU professor who's daughter is having a torrid affair with a local black?" All Will could utter was, "Ohh, shit!" His words came from deep within as he uttered, "I'm sorry, Mark. I had no idea that was..."

"That's who it is."

"Damn, Mark, what..."

"I should have told you a long time ago, but...You know me, Will. The color of the boy doesn't bother me in the least. He could be yellow, red, orange, or pink. The problem is that the son-of-a-bitch is using my daughter. He no more loves her than a fox loves a porcupine. And, why Regina loves him is beyond my comprehension." Mark shook his head and laughed sardonically, "Every time I see her, she is carrying one of his little bruises. I guess they are reminders of how much he loves her. My daughter, as you well know, Will, is very intelligent, and he is one step above the mentally retarded. If he truly loved her, I mean really loved her...I could accept the situation. But..."

"God damn it, Mark. Who is he? I know every black family in this county."

"If I told you, you would leave this bar, and you would forget Mrs. Wilkins at the hospital, and you would go to this boy's home, whip his ass, and throw him into the river…I can't let you do that, my friend. And that is the main reason I haven't brought this problem to your attention. However, I couldn't hold it back any longer. I had to confide in someone, and that someone was you."

Frustration was building up in Will. Mark could see it written all over his face. In a defeated tone, Will asked, "Is there anything I can do?"

Mark reached across the table with his scotch glass and clinked it against Will's glass of tea. "You are doing it now, Will, by just being my friend and my sounding board. Thanks."

Both men moved into the quiet zone and for some moments stared out the glass patio doors. The sun was close to the horizon. Some of the evening patrons were beginning to arrive for the Inn's happy hour. Still looking out toward the patio and swimming pool, Will softly asked Mark about his youngest daughter, Theresa.

"What about, Theresa?" Will knew that the presence of his youngest would help him combat the depression of his oldest. "Is she coming over this summer?"

"Gloria is allowing her to visit me for two weeks before her school starts." Finally, taking his eyes off the setting sun, he turned and faced his friend, "And if you work it right, two weeks can be a lifetime."

Laughter and loud conversation were now coming from the bar. The night was getting ready to play its first hand. The bar telephone rang, and Casey answered. He did his best at yelling out over the assembly at the bar, "Dr. West-more, it's for you. It's the hospital!"

Will rose and patted Mark on the shoulder, gave him a brief squeeze, and headed for the phone. His phone conversation was very short. He hung up the phone, shook a few hands of some of the townspeople at the bar, kindly refused their drink offers, and returned back to Mark. "Mrs. Wilkins is about to sin-gle-handedly change the population of Earth! Needless to say, my dear friend, I have to make my usual quick exit." Will took a quick sip of his iced tea and started to head toward the lobby of the Inn. "I wish I could be with you this Fri-day night at that singles party at the country club, but I don't think my wife would approve." Mark managed to smile and gave a high sign to his departing friend. Just before Will made his exit from the bar, he shouted back at Mark, "Don't forget your exam next week!"

*   *   *   *

Heavy, swagged, deep ruby-red, velvet drapes framed each window of the main banquet room of the Magnolia Country Club, and each window managed to overlook various areas of the magnificently manicured golf course. Once the sun set, everything of any importance took place within the elaborate, highly decorated building that had been the subject of numerous articles in *Southern Living*. The main building of the Magnolia Country Club had once been a grand specimen of the "ideal Southern plantation" from the Civil War era and made famous in *Gone With the Wind*. Very little of the original house remained. It had undergone numerous renovations, alterations, additions, and modernizations.

The enormous banquet room for this evening's activity, The Singles' Summer Regalia, was packed and swinging to a live band blaring out music from the 50's and 60's. The club's air conditioning system was taxed to the limit. Professor Mark Phillips was standing at the bar enjoying his favorite beverage. The bar was decorated with granite busts of various ancient Greeks and Romans and visibly supported by Corinthian columns. Marty, the regular club bartender, was working the main bar. Two portable bars had been set up inside the banquet room and were manned by temporary servers. Marty had just finished loading up a tray for one of the waitresses to carry into the main dancing area and finally had a moment for conversation. Mark was the closest customer, and one that Marty knew quite well. "So what do you think of the singles' party, Dr. Phillips?"

"If one could get past the conversations about former husbands, deprived children, alimony payments being late or too meager, child support problems, and constantly talking about the negative things in life, it might be a good party," was Mark's reply.

"You think you have heard some sad stories at this party? You ought to be behind this bar five or six days a week!"

"There must be five women to one man at this event. Where do they all come from?" said Mark.

"For this event, they crawl out of the woodwork. I'll bet that many of them are down here from Tennessee. Not too far to our north, as you know."

A very attractive woman, standing at the other end of the bar, was listening to the conversation of the two men. A slight smile was visible.

"It's really interesting, Marty. I've been dancing for about two hours with many hot, horny women and not one, as of this hour..." Mark glanced at his watch, "has made any kind of overture that they might be interested in a sexual evening. At least one could have been a bit tempestuous during a slow dance." Marty agreed. As they continued their conversation, the sophisticated, attractive lady at the end of the bar crossed to Mark's side. She tapped him on the shoulder, got his attention rather quickly, and proceeded to whisper something in his ear. She then moved away from Mark and headed toward the front door. She moved

like a professional New York model walking down a show runway. Every movement was sensual, and each step toward the front door was an invitation to a
show.

Mark turned back to Marty, whose mouth was open, and whose eyes were
fixed on the departing lady. "See you later, Marty, I just had an offer I can't
refuse. If I did, you would have to send out invitations to my funeral." Mark
quickly held up his scotch and soda glass, took a quick sip, made a toast to Mr.
Limburger, his favorite rat, and departed the Magnolia Country Club.

*   *   *   *

The summer of 1976 passed rather quickly for Mark Phillips. June and July
went by like quicksilver in an hour glass. The passing of time for the locals of
Magnolia, Georgia, was sometimes recorded by the passing shadows of a sun dial,
the coming and going of various insects, and the color changes in the local flora
and fauna, especially the leaves of the majestic maple trees that populated the
area. The passing of summer, for the immediate neighbors of Mark's bohemian
garage apartment, could have been an adventure for any diarist by simply counting the various makes and models of vehicles departing his driveway at different
times of the mornings on different days of the week. The models ranged from
Cadillacs to Fords, from sport cars to vans and trucks. Their owners ranged in age
from the low 20's to the mid 50's. Mark, during one of his lunch meetings with
Will, had mentioned that his summer escapades were very healthy, physical ways
of doing research for his book.

The first week of August was showing on the calendar, and Mark Phillips was
in his office at NGSU preparing for the upcoming fall semester. His office door
was open, an invitation for his department head, Dr. George Wessel, to occupy
the entryway and strike up a conversation. Wessel flipped through a handful of
papers and stopped on one particular paper.

Holding up the sheet of paper for Mark's examination, he said, "I see here that
you offered a double scholarship in English and Journalism to that Adena girl
from Albany."

"Certainly did. Her S.A.T. scores, transcripts, and references were outstanding. Just between you and me, George, I can't figure out why she selected North
Georgia State University. She could have been the star at any Ivy League school."

Dr. Wessel took a few steps into Mark's office. "That's easy to explain. The
Dean was telling me the other day that Adena's mother, father, grandmother, and
grandfather all attended this institution. One of her sisters managed to get

through two years here before dropping out to get married. Her father, I might add, is one of the richest men in Georgia. Made his millions, and still is, in computers…computers. Make no mistake, they are the machines of the future. How is your new book coming along? Your first one put our university on the map."

Mark leaned back in his chair, and a smile crossed his face, "Between you and Salina…you both would have me at the typewriter twenty-four hours a day!"

"Speaking of Salina, where is she now?"

"She and Barry are still cruising around the islands of the Caribbean."

"What an adventure. And, Regina? Is she still planning on going into the Army?"

"I really don't know the answer to that one, George. I wish I did. What I do know is that Theresa will be with me in two days. I've missed her terribly."

Dr. Wessel stepped back out the door of Mark's office, "Have a great time with your youngest, and enjoy the last three weeks of vacation. Give my best to your daughters."

Mark got up from his desk and followed his department chairman into the hall.

"I'll do that, George. And you do the same."

Mark had passed the self-service gas station at least a dozen times since enjoying his eggs, bacon, toast, coffee, and cheese grits at one of the town's popular greasy spoons. The supper hour was drawing close, but, number one, he needed gas, and number two, he wanted to make sure that Regina was working at the cashier's window. Finally, at a little past six, he saw her at the window and pulled his little Falcon to the first open pump. He filled up the tank and crossed to the window. He did not look at his daughter but kept his eyes on the money he was taking out of his wallet. Regina spoke first, "How are you, Dad?"

"I'm doing okay. How about yourself?" His eyes were still resting on his wallet.

"As good as can be expected."

"I'll make this short. Your little sister will be visiting me in a couple of days." He took a long pause and continued, "Will you take her back to the airport like you did last summer?" He could feel the tears beginning to cloud his vision.

"Yes, sir. Just give me a call. I'm at the same number. If possible, I'd like to spend a day with her." Once again, there was a long pause.

"Maybe."

Regina gave her dad back his change from the gas purchase. Mark still had not made eye contact with his daughter. "By the way, Salina said to tell you goodbye, that she loves you, and will see you first thing when she and Barry return. She said that you will understand." A few tears finally broke loose and moved down Mark's face. He turned his face slightly away from the window.

"Dad?" You know, you could come by here more often. I haven't seen you for nearly three months."

"The gas is lousy, and we really don't have much to say to one another, do we? We talked ourselves out last summer and didn't get anywhere. What is the situation with you and the Army?"

"If I go, I'll leave for basic training sometime in January."

Mark's heart almost stopped when he heard the "if."

"I'll call you." Tears were flowing as he moved away from the window. He took a couple of steps and turned back to face his daughter. Regina's face also showed streams of tears. Mark saw desolation and sorrow. Before making his departure, he managed to speak what was resting so heavily on his heart, "I love you."

As Mark turned toward his car, he heard Regina shout from the window, "I love you, too, Daddy!"

*   *   *   *

The Atlanta International Airport was always bustling with travelers. It was the hub for numerous airlines, national and international. It was also an easy place to get lost if you are in a hurry or you don't take the time to read the direction signs. Mark fell into both categories. As he finally arrived at the gate where Theresa would appear, he bowed his head and said a silent prayer thanking fate or whomever or whatever that made him decide to arrive at the airport a few hours early. Had it not been for a kind airline employee, he could still be standing at a United Airlines gate instead of a Delta.

Theresa, Mark's youngest daughter, received a bit more attention, adoration, and love than Regina or Salina. Mark would never admit to that, but that was the way it was. She had been the child to experience the agony of divorce, the innocent one, the one who could not understand why her mother and father could not simply solve their differences and get back together, back to the way things were. She had been ripped out of Mark's life by an edict of the courts and, by that same edict, allotted so much time out of each year to spend with him. The custody trial still seared his brain every time the memory of it was rekindled.

Her plane was on time! Mark spotted her as she made her way through the arrival area. When they both made eye contact, each made a movement toward the other. For Mark, it was a few steps. For Theresa, it was a run until she pounced into his arms.

With his arms wrapped around her, he managed to speak words that came from the depths of his heart, "I love you...I love you...I've missed you from my life—so very much."

She whispered into his ear, "I've missed you, too, Daddy."

They broke their embrace, and Mark held his daughter at arm's length. "You've gotten prettier, grown at least an inch or two, and...God! You've even started to develop a bosom!" They both started to laugh. "Let's go retrieve your bags and then get busy ending this summer with a bang and making up for some lost time. And before I forget it, Regina gets you one day next week. And, for that one day, I'll be able to regain my strength and catch a second breath." Arm in arm, they started walking down the busy corridor leading to the main hub of the airport. Masses of people were passing them in both directions.

"I thought you wouldn't mind making our first adventure stop at Six Flags Over Georgia. Our reservations have been made, and the great thing is, its not far from here. I was told that they would be having a nationally known rock group appearing there tonight." He looked at Theresa and noticed not only was she about to ask a question but that she had a few more extra freckles on each side of her nose.

"Don't ask me the name of the group. You know me: I think they're all alike. Noisy, noisy..." A jet flew over, drowning out the remainder of Mark's words.

As they continued their exit down the corridor, they locked arms and began a dance step. People behind them could have mistaken them for the Scarecrow and Dorothy dancing down the Yellow Brick Road.

The time went fast. With the exception of sleep, every moment was filled with activity. They initiated their special time together with a visit to Six Flags over Georgia and then traveled to the mountains of Tennessee for a six-day camping and fishing expedition. They trekked from the north of Georgia to its southern tip and spent a few days at St. Simons' Island, swimming and horseback riding. During this time, Mark discovered that Theresa was normal; she was thirteen going on twenty-two! Considering her normal development, he was also aware that she, like her sisters, was cultivating a keen intellect.

After Theresa's one day with her older sister, Mark took her to one of the exquisite state parks located in north Georgia, not too far from Magnolia. They had been there many times in the past, which made for a secure, identifiable location to say goodbye to summer, 1976.

The sun was making its last rays of sunlight visible to all the people in the park. The rays of color, ranging from purples to lavenders and from ambers to yellow, came shooting out from behind the distant hills like shafts of light from gigantic carbon arch spot-lights

A folk music group was on the stage of the outdoor amphitheatre and was leading the assembled crowd of campers in a sing-along. Mark and Theresa were joining in. When the song ended, Mark quickly turned to Theresa and said, "Let's go catch a better glimpse of the sunset down at the edge of the lake. It will be our last until next summer."

Theresa said, "Race ya to the beach! The last one there is a crusty crab!"

They both took off running around the amphitheatre and headed towards the lake. The folk singing could still be heard as it wound its way through some tall Georgia Pines.

Theresa, whose legs were much shorter than her father's, was the first to hit the beach. She shouted back at her Dad, "If I'm not mistaken, I see a crusty old crab heading this way!"

Mark finally made it to the beach and plopped. His breath was short, and his chest was reaching its boundaries. Theresa rushed to him and knelt by his side.

"Are you okay, Daddy?!"

Between gasps of air, he gasped, "Sure I'm okay, you little fink.... I'm going to put some sand on your nose." Mark grabbed Theresa, and they both wrestled on the sand. Mark spun her over and gently poked the tip of her nose into the sand. Both began to laugh.

"I'm a rusty *old* crab am I?"

"A handsome *old* crab. I forgot to add that." Mark was still holding her nose close to the sand, "Peace?"

"Peace."

Mark released her, and they both leaned back on the sand and looked at what was left of the sunset. Folk singing could still be heard coming from the park amphitheatre.

"I don't like the idea of saying goodbye tomorrow. It seems like you've been with me for only an hour or two."

"Next year will be different, Dad."

"You're thinking about changing addresses?"

"I've given Mom three years. It's now your turn...and my turn.... Dad?" She rolled over on her side. "Do you think Regina will ever leave that black guy?"

"Someday.... Someday she will walk away."

"The singing sounds great!"

"Want to go back?"

"No." Theresa reached out her hand and placed it on her father's, "Let's just lie here, look at the stars, and soak it all in." And with those words, the summer of 76 came to a close.

CHAPTER 5

▼

"Age does not protect you from love, but love to some extent protects you from age."

—Jeanne Moreau

Mark was busy typing up research he had completed before Theresa's arrival. Now that she had returned to her mother, the emotional turmoil had ebbed, allowing him to get back to work on his book. With each cup of coffee, or each scotch and soda, Mark would look at his research and question himself about the importance or validity of his work. His first book was purely classroom academic; however, a book about love down through the ages seemed adventuresome and full of challenges. "A bit ironic," he thought, "to be writing about something I've never experienced, or have I?" He still hadn't quite figured out what he and Gloria had experienced. He knew that in the beginning their relationship was quite sexual and biologically very electrifying, but what about those inner feelings that move through the mind and excite the soul, like those experienced by Gibran and his first love. Where were they? He was deep in thought when the phone on his desk quickly brought him back to the present.

Dr. George Wessel was on the phone, "Say, Mark? I hate to bother you but I have called four or five other faculty, and no one is home. I need some help moving into my new office. I hate to ask, but could you loan me your muscles for about fifteen or twenty minutes?"

Mark glanced at his typewriter, shrugged his shoulders, and thought to himself that age seems to enrich certain products; maybe the same principle applies to written works. "Once again my creative effort can wait, especially for my department chairman. He might even think about giving me a raise."

"Okay, George, I'll be right over. I hope you will forgive my appearance. I haven't shaved since Theresa left, and I look pretty scruffy."

"This operation doesn't have anything to do with beauty or appearance, Mark. Just warm up your muscles on the way over."

"Just give me a few minutes to jump into my overalls, and I'll be right there. I don't think the administrators would favor me running around in the hallowed halls of NGSU in my Fruit of the Loom underwear."

As Mark drove across campus, he was reminded that fall wasn't far away. Not only were the leaves on the trees beginning to change color, but so was the campus. The latest fall colors and fashions could be seen on the young students rushing here and there across campus. For the incoming freshmen, the old adage, "First impression is a lasting impression," certainly held true, especially for sorority and fraternity rush.

*   *   *   *

"My God, George, what is this desk made of? Lead?!"

George started to laugh. "Don't make me laugh, Mark, or we'll never get this damn thing through the door!"

Both men of the academy looked like a couple of school janitors as they wrestled, trying to manipulate a huge heavy desk through what both men imagined was one of those small doors in <u>Alice in Wonderland</u>.

Just as they managed to get half of the desk through the door opening, Adena Rutherford walked around the hall corner and approached the moving desk. She spoke to Mark's back.

"Excuse me? Could you tell me where Professor Phillips' office is located?"

Mark managed to slightly turn his smashed face toward Adena. As he did, his nose and the back part of his head got stuck between the desk and the door jamb; however, he did manage to answer Adena's question.

"Take the first left down the hall…" Adena started to chuckle on the inside at the squashed hairy face in the door. "His office is the fourth one on the right." Mark could barely see Adena's face.

Adena started to move down the hall but not without saying, "Thank you."

Dr. Wessel's voice came from the other side of the desk, "Mark? How come you…"

Mark got his face unstuck and answered, "How come I didn't talk to her?"

"Yes."

"Well, for one thing, my face got stuck between this Goliath of a desk and the side of your door opening. This damn thing is too heavy to stand here and hold. If we're not careful, we could be bowlegged for life!" George started to laugh. They both gave the desk one more tug and pulled it into the office. They immediately lowered it to the floor. Mark leaned across the desk, "Furthermore, if that young lady is looking for me now, she will be looking for me next week...And, next week is when I am scheduled for office hours and counseling. As of this moment, and no one would realize it, I'm still officially on summer vacation."

"Thanks, Mark, for your help and time. I know I probably pulled you away from working on your book." Attempting to jest with Mark a bit, he continued, "I might even request a pay raise for you."

$$* \quad * \quad * \quad *$$

The city of Magnolia, Georgia, was undergoing its annual, instant population explosion. Its streets were becoming overcrowded with parents and students, new and old. The local Holiday Inn, along with other motels around town, were overflowing. The Purple Passion was pulsating and celebrating a new academic year. Dorms and surrounding apartments were welcoming their new residents, and some of the returning students were holding welcome back parties throughout the city. Friday night in Magnolia was finally alive with celebration and merriment. One huge party, held by students from the English, journalism, and drama departments, was attempting to cry out to the locals that things were returning back to normal. Most of the faculty and students attending the party were of the old guard. Invitations with maps had been sent out to all new students declaring a major or minor within the departments represented. One room in the house was, as usual, dedicated to dancing, and disco music was blaring. No one was in the room. Most everyone present were busy in conversations about their summer adventures or lack thereof.

Carol Finley, one of the students hosting the party, was moving through the crowd when the front doorbell rang. She was one of the main greeters for the evening. Carol flung open the door. Adena was standing on the porch looking somewhat like an Amish girl that had gotten lost. Adena's hair was up in its typical bun. She was wearing her thickened glasses. Her make-up was sparse, and her dress hung loose to her ankles. Carol took what for her was a prolonged look at the new arrival but didn't lose a beat in her practiced welcome.

"Hello!" She extended her chubby hand to Adena, "I'm Carol...Carol Finley. My friends call me Heavy Hanna. You can call me whatever comes to mind. Welcome to the English, Journalism, and Drama Fall Kickoff Party!" She ushered Adena into the hallway,

"How was that for a greeting?"

Adena managed a weak smile, "Well, I know for sure that I'm at the right house." She folded the map she was carrying and quickly slipped it into her purse. Carol gently grabbed her by the arm and started to escort her into the party. "You've got to be a new kid on the block."

"I'm a freshman," was her reply.

Carol said, with a slight smile, "A freshman?! You could have fooled me!"

She always made that comment. She figured that it made the freshmen feel better about being newcomers. "Well, welcome aboard! Before we hit the warm bodies in the next room, you've got to tell me your name."

"Adena Rutherford."

"Welcome to NGSU, Adena Rutherford. What's your major?"

"I will carry a double major in English and journalism."

"Wow! A double major! I'm doing my best just to get through one. Mine's drama. Maybe you guessed it already. Anyway, hold yourself together." They were about to enter a noisy room off the hallway. Just to the right of the door hung a large metal pot and a solid metal spoon. Carol reached up and removed both of them from the wall. "These little items are our attention getters." When they entered the room, Carol began aggressively hitting the bottom of the pan with the metal spoon, and she and Adena were given immediate attention. They went from room to room, with Carol making the same announcement in each.

"Ladies and gentlemen, and I use that term loosely, may I have the privilege of introducing Miss Adena Rutherford. She is an incoming freshman and will be majoring in English and journalism." Following Carol's introduction, Adena would make the rounds of all the people in the room, shaking hands, introducing herself, exchanging names, majors, and usually which year of college each person was in. In some rooms, communication and introductions were kept to a minimum with simple waves of "Hello" and shouts of "Welcome."

In the last room, Carol, before banging the pan, turned to Adena and asked, "Who is your assigned advisor? Maybe he or she is at the party tonight."

"Professor Mark Phillips."

Carol did a double take! "Wow! Did you make out or what. Follow me. We just happen to be in the right room." She escorted Adena through the crowd and to the spot where Mark Phillips and Susan Wells were standing in conversation.

"Excuse me, Professor Phillips?" She quickly acknowledged Susan with, "Sorry for interrupting, Susan." Carol really wasn't sorry; she was just being nice to a fellow classmate, and anxious to finish all of the introductions. "Professor Phillips, I'd like you to meet one of your new advisees." She grabbed Adena's arm and moved her in front of Mark. "Her name is Adena Rutherford."

"Thanks for bringing her over, Carol."

A surprised look came over Adena's face, and she began to laugh. Mark turned his attention to the laughing girl in front of him.

"You're the Adena Rutherford from Valdosta. Welcome to NGSU." Adena tried to suppress her laughter, but it became even more robust.

Mark glanced at Susan, shrugged his shoulders, and turned back to Adena.

"May I share in your revelry?"

Adena managed to capture a moment of composure and answered, "Please forgive me, but...but...the other day, in the hallway, I thought you were a janitor. A janitor with a squashed face."

Mark joined in her laughter, "That's right, you came by early in the week to see me, and you did see me while I was helping my department chairman move a mountain into his office. At the time, I was unshaven and had my head stuck between the mountain of a desk and the side of a door opening." Mark could now picture the scene that Adena observed. His laughter increased, "I can easily understand your erroneous identification."

"Please for..."

Mark interrupted her with, "Miss Rutherford...you are forgiven. Allow me to introduce you to Miss Susan Wells."

Susan and Adena shook hands, "Welcome to the club, Adena." There was something unusual about the handshake. It was almost foreboding, but Susan tossed it off as soon as one of her favorite disco songs came from the dancing room. "Listen, that's one of my favorite disco numbers." She grabbed Mark's hand, "Let's dance." Susan started pulling Mark toward the dance area. "Come on and join us, Adena. Grab hold of any male that looks available!" They disappeared into the dance room.

Adena watched them leave. She looked around for Carol, but Carol had abandoned her to take care of her assigned duties. "However," she thought to herself, "Carol was absolutely correct when she said, "Wow, did you make out." Professor Mark Phillips, when his face wasn't being flattened between a wall and a desk, was one of the most attractive men she had ever met.

*   *   *   *

The faculty meetings had exhausted themselves. Mark could never understand the numerous meetings before the beginning of a new academic year. Not only were they redundant, but they devoured valuable creative time. For a new, incoming academic, the meetings might serve a purpose, but for those who had been teaching for a year or more, they were a total waste of time and energy. He thought that someone should disseminate new information to the returning faculty in an office memo and call off the meetings. However, meetings and more meetings were the way of the academic world. Mark was glad that the meetings ended, and he could start a one-on-one rapport with the students. He had been working in his office since early in the morning and actually enjoying every minute of the day. A student in his junior year was sitting in front of his desk.

"There you are, Stan." Mark handed him a fistful of papers, "You are now ready to register. You've selected some tough courses, but I'm sure that with your high GPA, you can handle the load." Stan rose and reached out his hand to Professor Phillips. "Thank you, Professor. I'll certainly let you know if I have any problems." He crossed to the door and made his exit just as Adena knocked on Mark's door and peeked into his office.

"Ahh, Adena. Come in. You are my last advisee of the day."

Adena entered Mark's office and started to sit down. Mark interrupted her movement.

"If you don't mind, Adena, considering that I have been tied up in this office since early this morning, I will grab what I need off of this desk, and I'll advise you while we walk across campus."

"Sounds great!"

"I've been told that it is beautiful outside, so let's go out and enjoy what's left."

Adena gestured toward the office door, "After you, Professor." Mark picked up the necessary advisee papers, crossed to the light switch, and guided Adena toward the hall.

He turned out the lights, closed his office door, and followed Adena out into the warm afternoon sunshine.

Students were everywhere, moving helter skelter from office to office and department to department. Most of them, like Adena, were being advised on what courses were necessary for them to graduate, how many hours of this and that, and once their papers were completed and signed by their advisors, they were ready for their first collegiate battle, registration. The typical summer humidity was nonexistent. Winds were moving in from the north, and evening temperatures were dropping down into the low 60's. The air was crisp, and Mark and Adena walked across campus toward the campus lake. Once there, they managed to capture a free picnic table and seated themselves.

"How is this for a rest spot?" inquired Mark, "This is a perfect location to observe all of the maple trees surrounding the lake. Just look at those brilliant yellows and oranges! They are certainly making a loud announcement that fall is not too far away."

"Very scenic," was Adena's short reply.

"I bring my classes out here on days like today, especially in the spring. Classrooms are stifling and claustrophobic at times. Don't you agree?"

"I agree."

Mark started to laugh, "Do you ever express yourself in more than three words?"

Adena turned her head away from Mark and looked out onto the lake. Her entire physiological system was in overdrive, and she couldn't understand why. What was different about this man now sitting across from her? Mark's question finally registered. She pulled her thoughts together and replied.

"Well...as this was my first advisement meeting...I was led to believe that one's advisor did most of the conversing. A student's place was simply to agree or disagree, approve or disapprove courses to be taken in a given semester."

"If that is the case, why didn't you bid me farewell when I signed and approved your course card back in front of the library building?"

"I'm not sure, really."

She began to chuckle softly, "Maybe I was waiting to be excused or something."

"Well, I'm glad we walked that extra mile. As I'm going to be your advisor for the next four years, our little excursion to this location will give me an opportunity to know you a little more. So, how did rush go? Were you accepted by one of the sororities?"

"Yes, I received seven offers and turned them all down."

Mark tried to hide the shocked look that he knew was on his face by turning slightly away from Adena. "You turned them down? But why, if you don't mind my asking? You have aroused my curiosity."

Adena finally turned her gaze from the lake to Mark, "I just felt that I would have to give up some of my independence. I've been under my mother's wing since I was born. I didn't want to crawl under another." Mark managed a smile.

"I've left the nest, Professor Phillips, and I plan to be as free as this..." she made a wide gesture with her arm, indicating all of the campus, "...institution will permit." As she spoke her last word, she jumped up from the table and ran down to the edge of the lake. Her quick movement startled Mark. Adena pointed across the lake.

"Some day, I want to be as free as that hawk."

Mark got up from the picnic table and crossed down toward the lake and stood behind Adena. "My, God! That is a hawk! I've never seen it around here before." Both stood in silence and watched the hawk circle in the air and finally disappear behind the maples.

Mark broke the silence, "Once you feel free to talk, you certainly move right to the point. However, I admire your candor."

Adena sat where she had been standing, and as she spoke, Mark sat beside her.

"I can understand why you like to come out here. It's very beautiful. And...I'm sure, lacking the invasion of students, this place could be quite serene."

"What are your goals, Adena? If you don't mind my changing the subject."

"I don't mind at all. Some day, I would like to be an editor. Not of a newspaper, mind you, but editor of a national publication. I really admire Helen Gurley Brown, especially for what she has done to turn *Cosmopolitan* around. But...most of all...I want to be a writer, one of the best. What do you think, Professor Phillips? Can this college teach me to be an outstanding writer?"

"You will receive the ground rules, the techniques, and the pressures. What you do with them will be up to you. A teacher can teach, but then again he can't. Do you understand?"

"You are correct. It's sort of like the old adage that you can lead a horse to water, but you can't make him drink. Now, Dr. Phillips, I would like to change the subject; that is, if you don't mind?"

"No."

Adena continued, "Would you be embarrassed if I asked you a few questions that lean slightly in the direction of sex?" Mark's face not only flushed, it was hot. It was too late to turn away, so he simply tried to stumble ahead. Adena, in the meantime, was smiling on the inside in response to Mark's reaction.

"Go right ahead with your...with your question...or questions."

"Well, while rush was on, I committed myself to attending a few fraternity parties. My first one was a total disaster. I sat the whole evening while these sex-craved frat rats practically attacked the girls I was with. I'm no prude, but I just happen to believe that sex and love are...or certainly should be, inseparable, a major point that separates me from Ms. Brown. However, we are at the main issue behind my jabberwocky. Dr. Phillips? Am I unattractive?"

Mark tried to get together his thoughts on this one. In all of his years teaching and advising, he had never run into this particular type of conversation. He didn't want to offend this young woman, nor did he want to lie to her. He was certainly in a quandary. He decided to give it his best shot.

"Adena, you are not unattractive. You might, however, fall into the category that some of the men use here on campus as a 'plain Jane.' I'm going to offer some advice, and it is not in the academic arena, and I pray that you will take it as objectively as I am going to give it. There are a few things that, as a newcomer to college life, you might want to change, not only for a greater enrichment of your campus social life but for your future goals…"

"I'm waiting," was her only reply.

Never had Mark felt so out of his environment. Even considering that he had three daughters, he felt like a Wyoming cowboy tending sheep.

"Should I list them?"

Adena was back to her one-to-four-word sentences.

"Please."

"One—Get rid of those old fashioned eye glasses or maybe the frames. Two—Do something modern with your hair. Three—Copy some of the make-up jobs pictured in *Cosmo*. Four—Get a little more fashionable in your wardrobe, if possible. You might admire Ms. Gurley Brown, but somehow you've missed a few things."

As Mark was going over his suggestions, Adena already knew about her shortcomings. What was sufficient for Albany, Georgia, and her high school years did not apply to this new episode of her life.

"You are absolutely right, Professor."

Mark breathed a sigh of relief, "I've made myself into a bookworm, and perhaps I've even used that as a means of escape." Adena stood up, and Mark did the same. "I've even hidden my hair—except from my closest friends. I will give your suggestions some serious thought." She extended her hand to Mark. "Thank you, Professor Phillips." As her hand touched Mark's, some kind of unexplainable tremor moved through her entire body. She immediately dropped his hand and continued, "Thank you…for a very enlightening advisement session. See you around campus." She turned and started to walk up the embankment of the lake. When she got to the top, she turned back toward Mark and shouted, "I admire your candor!"

Mark's eyes followed her until she disappeared. He had a lingering smile on his face and sensations were going through his body that he couldn't quite explain. He reached down and picked up a flat stone and turned back to face the lake. The sun was just disappearing from view. He looked in vain for the hawk. To bring a period to this day, Mark reached back with his arm and threw the flat stone across the top of the lake. It skipped four times on the top of the water, and, like the hawk, disappeared.

*   *   *   *

Like the song from the musical *The Fantastiks* the next time Mark and Adena would meet would be "Deep in September." Autumn had taken over, and sweaters and jackets were in. Mark had gone to the library to pick up some books that he had ordered from the University of Georgia. Most of the books contained information on love customs of the ancient civilizations, books that he could not obtain from his campus library. As he left the library, he passed right in front of Adena. Her transformation was nothing short of miraculous. She was now a beautiful young woman. When Mark passed her, she called out to him as he descended the library steps, but it was apparent that he did not hear her, so she followed him and yelled out again, "Professor Phillips! Professor Phillips!" By her third call, she had caught up with him. He turned to face her once he recognized her voice. He was so astounded by the new Adena that a few of his books fell out of his arms and scattered on the ground.

"Adena! Why…"

Adena smiled and turned as if she were modeling just for him.

"Do you like?"

"Do I like? You're a new woman, and…a beautiful one I might add."

Adena smiled as Mark bent over to pick up his books.

"Let me help you." Adena helped Mark to restack the books into his arms.

"Thank you for the compliment, Dr. Phillips…Might you have a few moments to talk or perhaps to advise?"

"With one so beautiful, I can find the time."

"Great! Can we walk down to the lake?"

"Certainly. But aren't you afraid we might freeze in this cold wind? I detest the first hard norther of fall."

"I'll bear it. Here, let me carry some of your books…Why so many old books?"

"I'm gathering research for a book that I'm attempting to write."

"Exciting! A novel?"

"Not exactly. It's a book about…love."

Both rambled on in conversation until they reached the lake. Quite a few students were gathered in different spots around the lake despite the cold breeze coming in from the north. The picnic table that Mark and Adena had occupied on their first visit to the lake was vacant, and they both crossed to it and sat in their original seats.

"Since I took your advice, I have attended another fraternity party."

"How did things go?"

"I received twelve propositions…I turned all of them down."

"Bravo!" was Mark's only response, and he couldn't figure out why he responded in such a fashion.

Adena's next question caught him totally off guard. "Why is sex so important, Dr. Phillips?"

Mark squirmed a bit on his bench and attempted to fight off his embarrassment..

"Well…ahh…for the fraternity boys, I would say that sexual accomplishment or seducements serve as a certain measure of manhood. I can't understand…"

Adena interrupted him, "It must make for a very narrow existence, or narrow vision, when a male boils life down to how many notches he can accumulate on his pole."

Mark cleared his throat and made a meek reply, "I would have to agree."

"And the girls," continued Adena, "Not all of them, mind you, but most, are just as bad as the guys. Sex, size, and body variation are the major topics of conversation. When a girl tabulates how many sexual encounters, how often, and how good, popularity is established."

Mark was hesitant but asked the question anyway, "How are you reacting to all this?"

"I haven't decided. I am, however, very curious about sex. And I feel very antiquated when I compare myself with my peers. I still happen to be a virgin."

Once again, Mark had to turn away from her because of his blush and embarrassment.

The topic was bothering him although he had broached it often with his own daughters; however, he found that discussing it with a new student to be very uncomfortable.

"Believe me when I say that being a virgin is certainly not a negative attribute. However, and I speak from experience with my two older daughters, losing one's virginity is not a negative in life. In your case, I would say that maintaining yours is an honorable choice." Mark wondered to himself whether he had gotten off the hook with that answer or had buried himself deeper into a quagmire.

"Maintaining my virginity has always been my belief. I was taught to hold that belief by my church and by my family. However, I've left the door open just in case I, to repeat, I, decide to shatter my entire upbringing. There's a student by the name of Eric Taylor. Do you know him by any chance?"

"Yes. I believe that he is president of TKE. And he is a very handsome young man. Quite a ladies' man I've been told."

"He has invited me out for tomorrow night. He will be introducing me to the Purple Passion. According to my roommate, he just might be the one to bring me into the twentieth century."

For the moment, Mark could not understand why he didn't mention to Adena that he and Susan, whom Adena had met at her first welcome to NGSU party, were also planning on being at the Purple Passion tomorrow evening. He also was bewildered by another feeling that he had never felt in his entire life: jealousy! They continued talking until the chill in the air brought the afternoon to a close.

*   *   *   *

The Purple Passion was rocking. The place, inside and out, was crammed with students and a scattering of young-to-middle-aged faculty members, male and female. The music was shaking the planking of the old building and causing the cracks in the walls to enlarge. Beer was flowing like water out of a busted hose.

The dance floor was packed, and it seemed that everyone was simply bouncing up and down with maybe a few side shakes here and there. Mark, aside from getting some good aerobic exercise, thought that, on the whole, opportunity for intimate contact and romance had been removed from modern-day music. He and Susan were in the middle of a bounce when he spotted Adena dancing on the opposite side of the dance floor. As he watched Adena move, he began to realize that for some people, modern music was appropriate and could be quite erotic. He couldn't help but concentrate on Adena. He knew that Susan would not notice that his eye contact wasn't on her. Disco dancing required body movement; eye contact was not essential. Mark noticed that Adena's date was also very interested in her movement. In fact, at one point, Mark thought that her male companion might be drooling.

The disco number finally ended, and as it did, a member of the rock group came forward to the microphone and made an announcement. He had to pause for a few moments while the crowd gave the band a robust applause.

"Thank you…thank you! Ladies and gentlemen! We have been rocking this place for almost an hour, but we have had numerous requests for the following song. So…in order to give the floor a chance to cool down, the band and I would like to slide into the next selection. Get close together for a song with lots of 'Feelings.' Shouts of approval and applause came roaring from the assembly.

Mark quickly turned to Susan, "Susan? Honey, do us a favor and," He pulled out his wallet and handed her some money, "go grab us two beers. I don't know about you, but that last marathon dance left me a bit thirsty. I'll meet you back at our table."

Susan took the money and turned in the direction of the bar, "You look like you could use a cold one...you're soaking wet." She disappeared into the crowd as the band began to play "Feelings." Mark started to leave the dance floor when his hand was grabbed from out of nowhere. To his surprise, it was Adena.

"Professor? May I have this dance?"

"Adena!"

"Surprised to see me?"

"Why...yes..."

Adena started to laugh, "Strange of you to say that. I could have sworn that you were watching me dance for most of the evening."

Mark pulled Adena close to him and, as always with a slow romantic dance, took her right hand and arm and placed them around to the curve of his back. Only their clothing separated the two. Mark started to join Adena in her laughter as he whispered in her ear.

"I was that noticeable, huh?"

"Yes."

"I ought to be ashamed of myself...but I'm not. I must say that you dance extremely well."

They danced for a few moments, each experiencing things happening inside their bodies that they had never felt before.

Adena was the first one to break the silence. Her mouth was very close to Mark's ear. "Would you believe me if I told you that I hate to dance disco or rock?"

"It would be..."

"My favorite singers are Andy Williams and Bobby Goldsboro."

"You, Adena Rutherford, are a surprising and very unpredictable young woman."

"And you, Professor Phillips, are a very smooth dancer. I thought for a moment that we were dancing on clouds." The slow music came to a close as Adena moved away from Mark, "I must return to my date, but before I leave, I must tell you that, you have a very nice warm body." Her last word, uttered with a smile, took her into the crowd and out of sight.

*   *   *   *

Six or seven weeks had passed since Adena had stepped foot on the campus of NGSU. The maple trees were nearly bare, and the first frost on the pumpkins had been recorded by the local farmers. Exam time was just around the corner in nearly all of her classes; consequently, on this particular evening, she was deep in study when her roommate rushed into the room like a whirling dervish.

Adena made a quick turn away from her desk, "What's going on, Rose?...My God, you nearly gave me a heart attack!"

Rose was out of breath, but she managed to blurt out, "Adena!...Adena!" She rushed across the room to her desk, "You've got to go to the journalism party tonight!"

"Slow down. I haven't missed a journalism party since I arrived on campus. However, tonight I must study for an exam coming up next week."

Rose caught her breath and leaped into her next comment, "Have you ever seen Susan Wells at a journalism party?"

"Susan, as far as I know, is not the intellectual type, nor does she cater to tea and crumpets. No, I have never seen Susan at a journalism party."

Rose rushed the next question, "And how about Professor Phillips?"

"I saw him once, right at the beginning of the semester."

Rose knew that she had a winner going with Adena's last statement, "Dr.Overstreet told me this afternoon that Dr. Phillips was going to be there this evening and will be talking about some of his *love* research!" Before Rose had a chance to finish her sentence, Adena was heading for the shower. Rose started to laugh as she asked the next question, "What are you doing?"

Adena cried out from down the hall, "Preparing for the journalism party!"

CHAPTER 6

▼

"Love rules the court, the camp, the grove, And men below, and saints above: For love is heaven and heaven is love."

—Sir Walter Scott

The party was over. The music for the evening had rotated between Mozart, Beethoven, Bach, and Rachmaninoff with a little Sibelius tossed in before the final goodnight. Once again the journalism party, usually hosted by Dr. Overstreet and his wife Nancy, accomplished another evening providing students and faculty with the opportunity to discuss academic achievements and trivia over martinis. Punch was provided for the students. Tea and coffee were available for those who did not indulge in alcoholic beverages. Cookies and dainty sandwiches were the main entrees. No one would come to a journalism party expecting to have an abundance of food. The word was out, eat before going or plan to eat after the party. Liquid refreshment took another direction.

A few of Overstreet's close friends were still lingering, and a few people were still drinking free booze. Adena was at the front door shaking hands with Dr. Overstreet and thanking him for another lovely party. Mrs. Overstreet was handing out coats and sweaters to various students and faculty who were departing for the evening. Adena stepped through the front door into a very cold, crisp evening. Mark received his coat and shook hands with Dr. Overstreet and followed Adena into the night air.

"Adena?"

She recognized Mark's voice. At the same time, it seemed like an electric shock moved through her entire body. She turned and replied, "Yes?"

"Do you have a ride back to campus?" He crossed down to her. They were so close that their condensed breath intermingled.

"No. I thought I would walk. It's only a mile or so. The night is so beautiful and just chilly enough to make you tingle with life." Adena knew that the tingle she was experiencing was not just from the weather; however, the feelings surging through her body were beyond her immediate analysis.

"I think I'm tingling a little too much," replied Mark, "and I suspect that you might be doing the same if you walk all the way back to campus. May I offer you a lift?"

Adena paused just long enough to give the impression that she wasn't in a hurry to accept the invitation. "Only if you throw in a fast-food stop." Mark laughed.

"I must have eaten a dozen of those small cookies."

"How about a pit stop at the local Pizza Hut?"

Adena grabbed Mark by the arm, "Where is your car?" She started pulling him in the direction he gave her. "A pizza! A pizza! My kingdom for a pizza!"

Arm in arm, they headed towards Mark's car. Both were laughing.

*   *   *   *

Adena's dormitory parking lot was packed with cars. Being a middle of the week night, most of the girls stayed in to study; however, many of the cars on the lot had fogged-up windows. Mark's little Ford Falcon was one of them. After finishing the pizza, Mark drove Adena to her dorm. Neither one of them wanted to leave the other, so a few hours of conversation ensued.

"...and that's my tragic story. I love my daughters. They alone have brought the sunshine along with a little rain into my life." He had completed the story of his life with his former wife and had filled Adena in on the backgrounds of each one of his daughters. It was the first time since his divorce that he had poured out his past to a female. Why to this particular female? He was trying to figure that out and not having much luck.

"You haven't said very much. I believe it has been my talking that has steamed up the windows. You're a very good listener."

"And you're a very beautiful person, Professor Phillips. I haven't said much because I was interested in what you were saying. A vast amount of what you told me corresponds with what I have heard since arriving on campus."

"I didn't know that I was that much of a topic."

"At this moment, you're considered somewhat of a playboy, a very eligible bachelor, a very renaissance-type of male and the most dynamic professor on campus. Not everyone is a teacher, writer, artist, poet, and lover."

Mark started to laugh, "I must have quite a reputation."

"That, my dear professor, is quite an understatement."

"Do me a favor, Adena?"

"Yes?"

"Please drop the 'Professor' or 'Professor Phillips.' Use them when it is proper to do so. Just call me Mark."

"That's a very good suggestion, Professor, whoop…I mean…Mark." She started to laugh.

"Now, it's your turn. You know a great deal about me, and I know so little about you except what I have gathered from references, letters, and transcripts. I do know your age. You're 20, soon to be 21. That puts you about two years ahead of the normal entering freshman. I'm assuming that your date of birth, October, kept you one year behind. The other year has me puzzled."

"You are correct Pro…Sorry. I missed another year of school in junior high because of a wicked case of mono. Insofar as my life, there is not much to tell. I have two wonderful sisters. One younger, one older. My oldest is married to a very rich farmer in South Georgia. A marriage, I might add, that was totally forged by my mother."

"By your mother?"

"My mother loves money, and she saw this farmer as an opportunity to add to the family coffers. My mother became a worshipper of money when she married my real father."

"I believe I've heard something about your father. Isn't he a millionaire?"

"Yes. In fact, my mother met him here at NGSU. His family was quite wealthy, and my mother was very beautiful. She used her beauty to capture the gold."

"If you're a sample of your mother, she must be a very attractive woman."

Adena barely got the word, "Thank," out of her mouth when a loud tap on the driver's side window thundered through the inside of the car. The light of a flashlight illuminated the window, but it was so fogged up that whoever was on the outside could not be seen. Mark quickly rolled down the window. Mulrooney, an elderly campus security guard, was standing outside the window peering in. Mark identified him right away, "Mulrooney? What's going on?"

Immediate identification went both ways. "Sorry, Professor Phillips! I had no idea."

Mark lightly touched Mulrooney's flashlight and moved the beam out of Adena's face. "Is anything wrong, Mulrooney?"

"No, sir. Just making my rounds like I do every night. It's one of my duties to check all the steamed up cars. Mulrooney was attempting to make an impression on Mark Phillips, the professor.

Mark had an idea that Mulrooney was fishing for a compliment, "You're a good, conscientious campus cop, Mulrooney. I'll report your diligence to Sgt. Powers tomorrow. Goodnight, Mulrooney."

With a smile, Mulrooney replied, "Good night, sir." Then he moved on to the next car, and Mark rolled up the window. Both he and Adena start to laugh.

"Wait until his story starts spreading around campus. Okay," Mark repositioned his knees toward the center of the car, and Adena did likewise. "Where were we before being interrupted?"

"I was about to thank you for your lovely compliment."

Mark was very intrigued about Adena's mother, especially with her approach to love and the necessity of money as a must in a love relationship. Mark wondered if money actually contributed to the enhancement of love.

"Tell me more about your mother. She sounds like a very interesting person."

"Well, my mother divorced Rutherford when I was six years old. The marriage didn't stand a chance from the beginning. It was founded on all the wrong reasons. Once the divorce was final, our real father stepped out of our lives forever. That is, except for his child support payments."

"Forever?"

"Forever. He never claims us as his children except on his income tax form at the end of each year, and he never once was present at any important event involving me or my sisters."

Mark felt deeply about Adena's loss of a father. To leave someone for many reasons, even simple incompatibility, is perhaps acceptable, but there were no reasons to abandon children.

"You mean, he didn't even attend your sister's wedding or your graduation?" To Mark, Adena's father's actions were incomprehensible.

"No. To him, we don't exist. My mother eventually remarried, and once again, for money. She married a very wealthy, first-generation, American-Austrian gentleman, who is very involved in the world of stocks and bonds."

"I'm very sorry…" Mark wanted to reach over and put his arm around her as he did with his daughters when they needed a positive touch, but he resisted. "It sounds like love, in your immediate family, runs a bit thin."

Adena's eyes, from Mark's vantage point, were beginning to mist up. How he wanted to touch her.

"Thank God for grandparents. They more than made up for the missing ingredient." Adena broke whatever barrier existed between them. She reached out her hand and gently placed it on top of Mark's. Her hand moved ever so slowly across his skin.

"Never stop loving your daughters, Mark. Never."

Mark once again was feeling something moving through him that he could not describe or even understand; however, he knew her touch was beyond any touch he had ever experienced.

"Believe me when I tell you that my daughters, all of them, are locked in the dungeon of my heart forever."

Adena knew that the conversation was getting way too personal and perhaps too emotional. She made an abrupt change in the topic and removed her hand from Mark's.

"Did you see those beautiful roses on Dr. Overstreet's front room table? They illuminated the room! Flowers take on such greater significance in the fall."

"Do you like roses?" Mark asked.

Adena expressed a soft laugh, "Show me a woman that doesn't. Yes, I love roses, especially yellow roses."

Mark had controlled his inner emotions and the turmoil, or whatever else was within him as long as he could. With great difficulty and a total abandonment of reason he said, "Adena? Would you mind my asking a very personal request?"

Adena noticed a change in Mark's voice. It was strained but softer and very compelling. In fact, when she answered him, her voice also took on a much softer tone.

"No."

"May I..." The pause seemed to last an eternity.

"May I...kiss you?"

Adena shut her eyes and instantly realized that she had been waiting for that question all evening long. Once again, she placed her hand tenderly on his.

"I would like that very much."

Mark moved closer to her and placed his free arm around her. Adena also moved closer to him. Their lips came together and touched without really touching. They lingered in that position for what seemed an eternity. Their breathing became synchronized; each breath became one. Finally, the lips compressed with complete tenderness and a softness that could not be matched. With the end of the kiss, there was silence as each regained composure or as much composure as could be expected. Mark was the first to break the silence.

"Did that feel like a...fatherly kiss?"

Mark was surprised by Adena's actions following his question. She rolled down her window, opened the car door, and placed one foot outside of the car.

"I must leave. I'm going home for the weekend. My sister Delores wants to see me. If it wasn't for her, I would stay right here. My ride leaves very early in the morning." She stepped out of the car, shut the door, leaned down to the window opening, and looked straight into Mark's eyes, "Your kiss was wonderful, and my body is telling me that it was certainly not a fatherly kiss. Good night. Mark Phillips, and thank you for a marvelous evening." She turned to go but immediately turned back to Mark, "By the way, Eric Taylor did not bring me into the twentieth century!" With that final remark, she disappeared into the dormitory.

Mark just stared out into the open space for a few moments then opened his window to let the late winds of September wrap around him. As he felt the winds envelope him, he turned to face the steering wheel and tapped his forehead against the wheel.

"What in the hell am I doing?" He started the car, and his last thought haunted him as he drove down the lonely road to his apartment and even lingered as he slid between the cold sheets of his bed.

*   *   *   *

The following evening, Adena was in Albany, Georgia. The only person she desired to see was her older sister. They had made arrangements to meet at their favorite mall and fast food restaurant, the Pizza Inn. They were both on their second or third glass of iced tea when Adena's conversation centered on Dr. Mark Phillips in general and the kiss in the car.

"…and my mind went into a tailspin! And my body, my very being, felt like something was trying to turn me inside out!"

Delores had never seen her sister so excited and yet so confused.

"You're speaking to the wrong person about love, Sis. Remember, our dear mother took that opportunity away from me and had me marry Joseph. I guess I'm learning to love the big galoot, but I can't give you any advice about what you are going through. If you think that's what your crazy, unexplainable feelings are leading to, then all I can say is, go for it!"

"Should I say anything to Mom?"

Delores immediately reached out her hand and grabbed Adena's. "For God's sake, no! Besides, everything that is happening is in the early stages of romance. Please take my advice, Sis, wait. Give things a little more time. Even if everything moves in the right direction…what about the difference in age? Have you thought about that?"

"What does age have to do with love and biology? Just look at Mom and Stan. There's nearly eighteen years difference between them, and that certainly hasn't stopped their bed from squeaking." Both girls broke out in laughter.

Delores knew her sister, probably better than anyone else in the family, and she was sure that Adena was in love. She also knew that anything or any advice offered would be useless now. Also, she knew that the best thing she could do for her sister, now and in the near future, was to be available whenever needed.

*   *   *   *

A Sunday afternoon at the Holiday Inn bar was a good way to escape any kind of crowd and occupy a rather quiet, secluded spot in Magnolia. Most of the visitors to NGSU had departed early in the morning. The church folk had accomplished their church-going for the day and paid their lunch-time visit to the Inn's restaurant, if that was on their Sunday list of things to do, so all was quiet in the town and in Casey's bottle and glass world.

Once again, Mark had called Will Westmore for an audience, and as always, Will accepted. Mark had spent the last hour telling Will about the past week and was finishing up with the car and Adena episode.

Mark paused after telling Will about the kiss.

"You think I'm crazy, don't you?"

"My God, Mark, how do you expect me to feel? She's only a couple of years older than Regina! Will had to smile and gave out a little chuckle, "Mark, you're nuttier than a Claxton Fruitcake, but thousands upon thousands of people throughout the world love that fruitcake, and I happen to love you like a brother."

Mark interjected, "Thanks, Will."

"Wait just a minute. I'm not through with you yet. It's my job to heal the sick and to make sure that people maintain healthy bodies. At the moment, I'd say that your body and mind are not quite in balance. The Yin and the Yang are upside down and, perhaps, even turned around. However…"

"I don't think I'm going through a mid-life crisis. This Susan I'm presently going with is only a year older than Adena. I don't see the age being a question. Do you?"

Will shook his head and chuckled at Mark's comment.

"Mark, my dear friend, as I was going to say, if you feel like you're heading for some-thing you have been looking for all of your adult life…continuing to pursue it would be the best prescription I could offer you."

"I hope you're right, Doc."

"Speaking about mind and body, damn it, if you don't come in for your physical, I'm going to slip an impotency drug into one of your scotch and sodas."

*   *   *   *

A number of roosters near Mark's apartment paid no heed to those who desired to sleep past the rising sun. Susan and Mark were in bed and sound asleep when the telephone rang, beating the local roosters to the punch. It rang a second time. Susan rolled over, reached over to the night stand for the receiver, and picked up the phone.

"Hello?...Hello?"

There was a long pause on the other end of the phone. Adena was hesitating to say anything. She knew who answered the phone, but the reality of the situation gave her an unexpected jolt.

"Is Mark Phillips there, please?"

Susan, still somewhere in the dream that was interrupted, managed to reply, "Yeah. Hold on for a minute." She turned with the phone in her hand and gave Mark a vigorous shake. "Phone call." She handed Mark the phone, rolled over, and retreated back into whatever could be salvaged of her dream.

Mark grumbled, "What time is it for God's sake?...Hello?"

Adena tried to make her voice as soft as possible, "There's a beautiful sunrise about to take place this morning." Mark immediately recognized the voice.

"If you can pull yourself away from your company, you might be able to catch it. I know that it will be inspiring and a great way to start off a Monday!"

"Adena?"

She paid no attention to his question but continued, "I'll be leaving a little surprise outside your office. It's the perfect size to fit between two bodies on a bed. See you later."

Mark sat up. The phone went dead. His head was still a bit fuzzy, and he was feeling a bit stunned. He crawled over Susan who had returned to her dream. Placing the phone back on the nightstand, he went to the kitchen, flipped on the coffee maker and crossed back through the front room to the porch door. As he stood on the small back porch landing, a smile came upon his face. Adena was correct. The sunrise was exquisite!

Later that morning, as Mark approached his office, his eyes searched for the surprise that Adena had said would be there. As he neared the entrance to his office, he spotted a small, strange object at the very base of his door. He reached down and picked it up. It was a little stuffed puppy. A small card hung around his neck. Mark opened the card: "This is Puff."

The 'stuffy' was small enough to nestle in the palm of his hand. It was beige with a short, dark-beige tail and dark-beige floppy ears. Its eyelids were dark-beige, complemented with deep black eyelashes. A black nose and a pink muzzle made him complete. Puff's arms were folded under his head, and he was fast asleep. Mark adopted Puff on sight. As he smiled at the little puppy in the palm of his hand, a familiar voice directly behind him broke the morning silence.

"You like my friend? I bought him on impulse, just for you."

Mark turned to see Adena standing in the hall. She was wearing a very alluring fall fashion outfit that clung to every fold of her body. The outfit complemented her youthful breasts, her thin waistline, and her voluptuous behind. It took Mark a moment to reply as he took in the sensuous beauty standing before him.

"You…made a good choice. I have just hired him as my personal bodyguard."

"I'm sure you've been outside this morning. We're having an Indian summer."

Mark opened his office door, turned on the lights, and crossed to his desk. Adena followed him into the office.

Mark looked at Adena over his desk and smiled, "I had a feeling the day was going to be beautiful and extra special. It started with a fantastic sunrise."

"Professor Phillips," she crossed to the chair in front of his desk and sat down, "I'm having a little difficulty in that Intro to Statistics class. The professor has a very pronounced nasal twang when he lectures and, at times, is very difficult to understand." Adena attempted a mimic of her statistics professor She held her nose and said, "The mean of this and the median of that will give you one helluva mess!" She looked straight at Mark, "Don't sit there and look like you don't understand!"

Mark broke loose with laughter. "Adena?"

"Yes?"

"How would you like to experience some of my gourmet cooking this evening?"

"Am I to understand that Miss Wells will not be there?"

Mark's face turned a light red, "She will not be present."

"Then, Professor Phillips, I couldn't think of a better way to spend a Monday evening."

Mark was still attempting to control his laughter, "We can discuss your statistics problem over supper. I'll pick you up at your dorm around six-thirty."

"If you wouldn't mind, I'll have my roommate drop me by your apartment."

"Well, at least someone is thinking around here. You will make an excellent politician someday, providing you ever move in that direction."

Adena stood and started to leave, "See you at six-thirty…. Should I bring anything?"

"Just yourself." Mark held Puff up in the air, "If he's guarding the door, just toss him a sleeping biscuit. He loves them."

That evening, Adena found herself sitting at a card table covered with a very beautiful linen table cloth. It was embroidered with pink roses and green stems and vines that moved along the outside edge. The table was appropriately set for a dinner for two. In the middle of the table, three candles were providing ample lighting, and by each plate stood a beautiful crystal glass covered with ornamental etchings. The light of the candles was bouncing off the crystal glasses and helping, with the assistance of music from the stereo, to set a very warm, romantic mood. This was all taking place in Mark's small front room. A room usually used for watching television and working on his book. Mark had outdone himself in cleaning up the front room. He yelled from the kitchen, "Dinner is almost ready!"

"It smells divine."

Mark entered from the kitchen and went to the table. He carried a bottle of wine and a long rose box.

"The tablecloth and the embroidery work once belonged to my grandmother. The wine glasses were also hers, both items that my ex managed to overlook. They have been in the family for many, many years." He sat the bottle of wine on the table and handed Adena the rose box.

"A little gift for you."

Mark sat and poured the wine. Adena opened the box and pulled out a plastic yellow rose. As she withdrew it from the box, a smile came across her face.

"That, my dear, is a prime example of life in a small college town. I remembered you saying that you loved yellow roses. Anyway, I searched this entire community for yellow roses. That is what I wound up with!"

Adena drew the rose close to her heart, "It's beautiful."

"I couldn't even find a silk yellow rose."

"And it's all the more beautiful because of the thought behind it."

"I figured that one would suffice. A bouquet would have been ridiculous." They both began to laugh.

Adena raised up her glass of wine, "A toast! Here is to my…Knight…Knight of the Yellow Rose!" As she finished her toast, the music of Andy Williams came from the stereo.

"You didn't forget a thing did you. Do we have time for a dance?"

Mark rose from the table and took her hand, "I believe we do." They crossed to the middle of the living room and once again their bodies came together. No space existed between them as they began to dance.

*   *   *   *

As the week progressed, Mark was confronted with thoughts and emotions he had never encountered in his life time. When he was lecturing by the lake, if he spotted Adena walking across campus, his lecture would falter. One day, at a faculty meeting, Dr. Wessel was going over some changes in the curriculum, and as he was speaking, all Mark could hear was, "And it's all the more beautiful because of the thought behind it." Dr. Wessel's voice seemed to get louder, but Mark couldn't make out his words because Adena's words were overpowering, "Your kiss was wonderful, and my body is telling me that it was certainly not a…" Dr. Wessel was standing beside Mark. His words finally had broken through, "Do you approve of that change, Mark?"

"…Why, yes…I believe it will be wonderful!"

Friday finally arrived. Mark was in the Student Union picking up a cup of coffee to take to his office. Out of the corner of his eye, he saw Adena heading in the direction of the bookstore. He grabbed the styrofoam cup filled with coffee and hastened after her.

"Adena!"

Adena heard him call her name and turned around just before entering the bookstore. As he approached, she waved to him and then looked around and noticed quite a few students standing close by.

"How are you today, Professor Phillips?"

Mark crossed to her, "Never felt better! How about joining me at a table?"

As they crossed to a table, Mark asked her if he could get her anything. Her answer was short and to the point, "I have time for just a short talk. My next class, with our favorite Dr. Nasal, is in five minutes. I was going into the bookstore to get an exam booklet, but my lined paper will do just as well.

"I'll be quick," replied Mark, "Are you going home this weekend?"

"No," She lowered her voice, "That means that I would like to spend some time with you."

"Do you like picnics?"

Adena reached under the table and gave Mark's knee a gentle squeeze and answered Mark's question. He made a slight jump at the unexpected touch.

"I **love** picnics!"

Mark took a quick glance around the cafeteria to make sure that no one was looking their way. He managed a smile.

"Be serious."

Adena laughed, "I was just teasing you; I looked around before I squeezed. Yes, I truly enjoy picnics. Why, do you have one planned that includes me?"

"You and some ants. How about Saturday morning? Free?"

"Free. You can pick me up outside the library at...?"

"Ten o'clock?"

Adena stood up and looked at her watch. "Gotta rush. See you at ten."

Mark watched her move through the cafeteria and out the door. Her perfume still filled the air, and her touch still lingered on his knee.

CHAPTER 7

▼

"Love sought is good, but giv'n unsought is better."...*Cyrano de Bergerac*

—Edmond Rostand

Shortly before his divorce, Mark had purchased several acres of land, approximately eight miles from downtown Magnolia. When he and Gloria ended their marriage, she opted for the new car, and Mark got to keep the land. He loved his own personal forest. He believed that he truly owned a spot on Earth where fairies, goblins, and leprechauns, if they really existed, could call home. His land was thick with pine and maple trees. The property was so heavily covered with trees that one could get lost if not familiar with the lay of the land. The maples had lost most of their leaves by the time Adena and Mark visited his little paradise. The Indian summer days enhanced the special aromas of late fall. The scent from the pine needles on the forest floor was predominant. It was late morning before the voices and laughter of Adena and Mark could be heard moving through this small, enchanted part of Mark's world.

Both were running through the trees and brush. Mark was chasing Adena. He finally got close enough to leap forward and grab hold of her thigh. They both took a tumble and fell into a pile of leaves and pine straw. Mark, gasping a bit for breath, admitted his weakness, "You're too fast for me."

She was laughing, "You wouldn't have caught me if I hadn't got caught in those briars back there."

They leaned back and nestled into the pile of leaves and pine needles. A ray of sunlight broke through the trees and enveloped them in warmth.

"So what do you think of my parcel of paradise?"

"It's beautiful. So serene and secluded from the world. I like that."

"Someday, I'm going to build my dream home right on the spot where we placed our picnic blanket."

"It's an ideal location. In fact..." Crazy pictures were flashing in and out of Adena's mind, "It would be a perfect location for an outdoor wedding."

"Do you really think so?"

Their hands moved across the blanket of leaves and touched and connected. Adena and Mark lay silent and motionless, trying to cope with the racing of their thoughts and the sensations that each was feeling. Adena broke the silence, still with eyes shut, but with her face aimed at the sun.

In a very quiet voice she asked, "Do you ever plan on marrying again?"

There was a long pause and a slight squeeze of Adena's hand, "Perhaps...someday." He moved onto his side and faced Adena. Her face was radiant from the sunshine. "If you don't mind my saying so, you're very beautiful in the sunlight."

Adena said "Thank you," and quickly rolled over on top of Mark, holding both of his hands and arms down against the earth. "Enough...my Knight of the Yellow Rose. Let's see the rest of your kingdom." She leaped up, cleared Mark's body, and took off running. She broke out of the forest onto an old rustic road. Mark was right behind her. They ran up a small hill. Mark stopped and ran off the road. As he did, he called out to Adena, "Adena!. Adena! Come here and look!"

Adena turned on the top of the knoll and ran back to Mark, who was standing in a large patch of fall wild flowers. Most of them were colored blue and purple, and their petals were enormous.

"Look at these beautiful creatures. They bloomed today, just for our visit!" He handed a bouquet to Adena, who was laughing and enjoying Mark's imagination. She placed some in her hair. The brilliant colors complimented her brunette hair, which hung below her shoulders in the front and cascaded to her waist in the back.

Mark stood silent for a moment. He was spellbound by her beauty. He moved to her and placed his hand beneath her chin. "You put to shame all of the fairies that occupy my kingdom." He quickly moved back to the road and did a few spins.

"Why, at this moment, do I feel like a crazy teenager? Do you think, my fair lady, these magic flowers are giving off some kind of aphrodisiac fragrance?"

With laughter in her voice, Adena responded, "Enough, enough, sir knight...With these magic flowers you should go into the florist business. They are affecting me. I'm getting lightheaded and a bit giddy."

Mark took off down the road and ran up the small hill. Adena was right behind him. As he descended the knoll, he moved off to the side of the road and started toward a ravine. When he approached the side of the ravine, he stumbled and fell into it. Adena, afraid that he might have hurt himself, ran to the edge and called after him, "Mark?...Mark?...Are you okay?" The sky was becoming darker, and thunder could be heard in the distance. Mark called out from the ravine, "I'm okay...You won't believe what I have found!" Reappearing from the ravine, Mark held aloft a small watermelon.

"The fall of the year, and I discover a watermelon! I do have a magic forest." He crossed to Adena, "It must have escaped the ravages of fall in that ravine. The frost landed on the pumpkin but went right over this little jewel. The warm Indian summer days might even be responsible for its existence."

Mark handed the little watermelon to Adena. She rubbed her hand across its smooth surface and gave it a thump with her finger. The melon returned the thump with a clear, deep, hollow, resonating sound. "It sounds like it's ripe," said Adena, "Do you think it will be good enough to eat?"

"Most certainly." Mark looked up at the sky, "But I think we'd better head back and transfer our picnic outing to the front room of my apartment. If we don't, I expect a very wet afternoon."

They had just made it back to their picnic area when the rain came pouring down. The picnic paraphernalia was rounded up in a hurry, and they both rushed to the car. Tossing everything into the back seat, they stared at each other and started to laugh. Both were soaking wet. Their laughter subsided, and their wet bodies came together. They embraced, their wet lips found one another and fused together. The kiss was long and electrifying for both. The wet condition of the two lovers broke the kiss when both began to shake from the cold.

Mark, concerned about Adena, asked if she were cold. Her reply prompted him to start the car and head to his apartment. Her reply was, "Hot and cold, take your pick."

Adena was sitting on the floor of Mark's front room. A dry picnic blanket had been spread out on the floor. On the blanket were sandwiches, wine glasses, and two bottles of wine. One was empty and the other half full. Candles lit the middle of the picnic blanket, and soft music was coming from the stereo. Thunder was still the major instrument being played outside, and the rhythmic pounding of the rain could be heard hitting the metal roof of Mark's apartment.

Mark entered from the kitchen carrying a small platter containing sliced, mouth-size pieces of the watermelon. He crossed to the blanket and handed Adena the platter. "This fruit, according to ancient Greek legend, was the favorite food of the gods." Mark sat next to Adena. "And to think that it was lying in wait of our visit." Mark reached over to the watermelon and handed Adena a slice and took a slice for himself. "Eat, my beloved, and join me in paradise."

The melon was cold, sweet, and juicy. Some of its nectar ran down the mouth of each participant. Their mouths, stained and moist from the reddish liquid, took on a very sexual appearance. Adena moved closer to Mark and made a very slow, turning movement and positioned herself across his lap.

"Mark, the wine and watermelon are making me very light-headed. And I think my body temperature is rising."

"I'm a bit intoxicated myself...but not from the wine or melon."

Adena moved her hand up to touch Mark's cheek, "From what, may I ask?"

Mark looked deep into her eyes, "Need you ask?"

Adena could feel the swelling in Mark's lap. "Mark, I am not going to hide my feelings any more...I think, or I feel, that I'm falling in love with you, and I'm frightened...What is love, Mark? Tell me." Her eyes were pleading. Mark was lost and thrilled at the same time, "Adena...I...I teach the subject. I'm research-ing it. I'm even writing about it, but...I can't answer your question. All I know is that for the past month, I have been confronted with, and wrestled with, feelings that I have never felt before. However, I have come to one conclusion."

"Yes?"

"I believe that I have fallen in love with you. Your face is with me every day, almost every minute. You are constantly in my thoughts and even in my dreams. When I was with Susan, I wanted desperately to be with you."

Adena stood up and reached for Mark's hand. No further words were spoken. She pulled him off of the floor, and they kissed, and the kiss was filled with all of the passions of human history. She led him across the front room, pausing only to turn up the romantic music coming from the stereo, and continued her path to the bedroom.

*   *   *   *

The following weekend, Mark, Adena, and at least two dozen students were holding a fund-raising car wash at one of the local filling stations. They were all staying busy because the temperature outside was hovering somewhere between 48 and 50 degrees Fahrenheit. The warm days of an Indian summer had deserted north Georgia. Aside from extra coats and sweaters, movement was the only way to stay warm. A couple of students managed to "accidentally" hit Mark with a spray of water. As they apologized, they couldn't control their laughter.

Adena was busy drying off one vehicle when, out of the corner of her eye, she spotted her mother and stepfather walking toward her.

"Mother!...Carl!" She dropped what she was doing and ran in their direction. She was quite surprised to see them. "What are you all doing here?"

Carl was silent. Her mother responded, "You haven't been home for such a long time, figured a visit was in order. Your dorm mother told us where we could find you."

Adena took her mother by the hand and gestured for Carl to follow them as she led them across the filling station driveway toward Mark.

"Mother, Carl, I have someone that I want you to meet." She called to Mark, and Mark, looking like he had just stepped out of a rain storm, stopped what he was doing and walked over to Adena. Soap bubbles covered just about every inch of his body. When he saw the two people with Adena, he immediately knew that he was about to meet her parents. As he got closer to Adena's mother, he knew right away where she had obtained her beauty. As Adena had mentioned, her mother was quite beautiful.

"Mother, I'd like you to meet Professor Mark Phillips. And, Professor Phillips, this is my stepfather, Mr. Carl Getz."

Mark reached out and shook their hands, "My pleasure. Adena has told me a great deal about both of you."

Adena's mother glanced at her daughter, "I'm sure she has."

Mark ignored the comment and continued, "I hope you will forgive my appearance, but the English club is trying to earn money for a trip to Atlanta."

Adena's mother was sizing up Mark. Even with the disheveled hair, wet clothes, and bubbles, Adena's mother could understand why Adena hadn't been coming home.

"One of the Atlanta theatres is producing *Cyrano de Bergerac*, a romantic classic. And, as you can see, these students are eager to see it…It beats having to read it…Well, if you will excuse me, I'll return to my little project." He turned to go, but was stopped by Adena's mother.

"Professor Phillips?"

"Yes."

"Hold to for just a moment." She turned and addressed Carl, "Carl, darling, give them something towards their project." Carl pulled out his wallet and handed Mark a bill.

"Thank you, Mr…ahh…Mr?"

"Getz," replied Carl with a strained smile.

Mark started to go but turned back with, "Glad to have met both of you." As he headed back to the car wash and his students, he sighed with relief. He glanced down at the donation he had received from Mr. Getz, and his spirits soared when he saw a one hundred dollar bill!

Adena's mother returned her focus to her daughter, "He's a very charming and attractive professor."

"He's one of my favorites."

"I'm sure he is…Please ask Professor Phillips to excuse you from this…this little exercise for a short while. Carl and I would like to spend some time with you."

"Wait for me over at the Holiday Inn. I'm assuming that that is where you all are staying. I'll join you there in about thirty minutes."

"We will expect you in thirty minutes." Adena's mother and Carl returned to their car and quickly disappeared down the road.

Adena rejoined Mark at the car wash, and the first thing to come out of Mark's mouth was, "Do you think that your mother…?"

"Yes," was Adena's immediate reply.

*   *   *   *

The light was dim, the table lit by one lonely candle. Across the ceiling were artificial grape vines entwining in and out of every niche and cranny, creating an almost solid canopy of green above the tables. Clumps of artificial grapes were protruding and hanging from various locations within the artificial greenery. The aroma of Italian cooking tantalized the senses. To make the assault on the senses complete, an Italian singer, playing an accordion, was moving among the tables, pausing here and there to personalize a song for any couple that looked like they were in love or wanting to move in that direction.

Most of Mark's college group had opted for Underground Atlanta where they could find fast music and fast food. Mark had made reservations at this particular restaurant before his group even left Magnolia. Reservations for two.

Mark took a slow sip of his wine and stared at the young woman facing him across the table. He retired his glass, reached his hand across the table, and placed it on Adena's. "How did you like the play?"

"'Like it' is an understatement. I loved it!"

"You are, or you are going to be, an incurable Romantic."

"I didn't like the ending. Why didn't Cyrano come right out and confess his love for Roxanne?" She shook her head, "He suffered so."

"But he was complete, at least he thought so. He was the perfect Romantic hero of the day and of the period in which the play was written."

Adena took her glass, moved around the table and sat next to Mark. She snuggled close to him with the words, "I loved the balcony scenes…" She looked into Mark's eyes, "Why can't men **woo** that way in the twentieth century?"

Mark thought for a moment and answered, "I really don't know. Perhaps our society has become insensitive or immune to the beauty of poetry and romance."

"Judging by the reactions of the females in the audience and in our group, and I include myself, the yearning for romance and poetry is still very much alive and desired."

As Adena concluded her comment, the Italian singer came to the table and began a romantic ballad, one taken right out of *Lady and the Tramp*. If Adena had wanted to snuggle closer to Mark, she would have had to become an appendage. They were as close to being one, in public, as humanly possible.

*   *   *   *

"Hey, Adena!" came a call from the hall. Adena's roommate showed up at the door. "I have to go and get some gas for my clunker. I thought you would appreciate a break from studying. You wanna go?"

Adena took a look at her books and agreed with her roomy. It was time for a break. "Okay, I'm with you. Maybe you could take a side trip for an ice cream moment?"

"Sounds inviting. Let's get going."

When they pulled into the filling station, Adena suddenly realized that it was the gas station where Mark's oldest daughter worked. Her roommate started to gas up the car, and Adena got out of the car and walked toward the cashier window. A girl fitting the description that Mark had given her of his daughter matched the girl at the cashier window. Adena wasted no time approaching her.

"Hello! Might you be Regina Phillips?"

"I certainly am," replied Regina.

"Allow me to introduce myself. I'm Adena Rutherford."

"Ahh, so you're the queen in my dad's life. I'm very happy to meet you. My dad told me all about you two just a couple of weeks ago. I was wondering if I was ever going to meet you."

"Well, you know that your dad avoids coming here. I wish that were not the case, but it is. When I realized this was where you worked, I came right over to the cashier's window. Now that I know where you work, I'll make it a point to accompany my roomy every time she has to gas up her car, and I'll make sure that she does it here."

Regina was immediately taken by Adena. She could understand why her dad had developed an interest in her.

"From what my dad said during his short visit here, you must be something really special. I haven't seen my dad this happy—ever."

"To hear that from you makes me very happy. If you don't mind my asking, how are things with you? Are you happy, Regina?"

Regina managed a weak smile, "I'm still searching for it, Adena."

Adena saw her roommate coming towards the cashier window and yelled out, "Don't worry about it! I've got it already! You can pay for the ice cream." Adena reached into her pants pocket and pulled out the money for the gas.

"Regina, I know that your father loves you deeply. Don't forget that. And, if you ever need me, here is my phone number at the dorm." She scribbled it quickly on the receipt. "I've got to rush, but believe me when I tell you that I will be back." She waved goodbye to Regina and returned to the car.

*   *   *   *

Mark, sitting at Will's bar, was about to finish his fifth scotch and soda. Will was behind the bar mixing Mark another when his two youngest boys came rushing into the den playing cowboys and Indians. A few shouts and a few verbal "Bang, bangs!" and they disappeared to another area of the house.

Will called out to his wife, "Say, honey, will you please keep the boys out of the den?"

From somewhere in the kitchen came his wife's voice, "I'll try, but I'm making no promises."

Will started to pour Mark's soda into the scotch glass he was holding when in walked his oldest daughter, Wendy, a college senior at NGSU.

"Hi, Professor Phillips! Excuse me for interrupting your conversation with Dad."

"That's quite all right, Wendy. For most of the evening, we have been caught in a crossfire between cowboys and Indians."

Wendy leaned across the bar and confronted her dad, "Dad...I need to use the car this evening. As you know, my car is in the shop for new brakes."

"Go ask your mother."

"I already have, and she said to ask you."

Will smiled and moved to the back of the bar, reached for the car keys in his pocket, and turned to Mark, "Nothing changes. I'll bet this little scene is the same in at least a thousand American households at this very minute."

"Dad?...The keys."

Will reached across the bar and handed Wendy the keys. "Be careful."

Wendy leaned over the bar and gave her dad a kiss on the cheek, "Thanks, Dad. I love you, and I will be careful." On her way out of the den, she said good-night to Mark.

Will turned his attention back to Mark, "Now, where were we? Ohh, yes, I was mixing you another drink. In fact, I'm holding it in my hand. The scotch is present, but the soda is lacking. Before I pour in the soda, are you sure you can hold another?"

"Just deposit the soda and slide it down this way."

Will poured the soda and slid the drink to Mark. "A couple more of those and I'll have to either tuck you into bed or drive you home."

"Damn, I'm glad that my favorite bartender is my best friend."

"You are very lucky."

"So, what do you think about what I've managed to tell you this evening?" Mark glanced around the den, expecting another cowboy and Indian attack.

"Do you want the truth, or something that sounds good?"

"Both."

"I love you, Mark. You know that."

"I know."

"First, if what is happening between you and Adena is making you feel alive for the first time in your life, as I have said in the past, reach out and grasp it. On the other hand, the age difference, as you well know, holds all of the elements for tragedy. So, I ask you why?"

"I'm getting into a poetic mood."

"You're getting drunk."

"Abide me. I'm getting ready to answer your, why. I may screw up the quote, but here goes:

I tell you,
There comes one moment, once—
    and God help those
Who pass that moment by!—
When Beauty stands
Looking into the soul with
    grave sweet eyes…."

Mark paused in an attempt at pulling together his faculties and his thoughts. Will popped open a beer and said, "I'm waiting. Is there more?"

"This is going to be a paraphrase attempt…" Mark held onto his drink and took a couple of steps away from the bar, and like an actor on the stage, turned to Will, took a bow, stood straight and began his lines:

My old friend—look at me.
And tell me how much hope remains for me
With snow covered ears! Oh, I have no more
Illusions! Now and then—bah! I may grow
Tender, walking alone in the blue cool
Of evening, through some college path
        strewn with flowers
After the benediction of the rain:
My poor autumn nose inhales
April…and so I follow with my aged eyes
Where some boy, with a co-ed upon his arm
Passes a patch of silver…and I feel
Somehow, I wish I had a love too,
Walking with silent steps under the moon,
And holding my arms so, and smiling.
Then I dream—and forget
And then I see my aged reflection in the pool of truth…"

Mark took a couple of steps toward his avid audience, and his friend, "I know this drama has the potential for a tragic ending, Will, but I'm willing to take the gamble."

"You know that I wish you nothing but the best. I'll be here for you no matter how the play ends."

Mark, with an excitement in his voice, crossed up to the bar and deposited his glass.

"Will? Do you have an old hat…and a yardstick that you could loan me?"

A puzzled look appeared on Will's face. "What in the hell do you want with an old hat and a yardstick?"

"I'm in the mood to do a little acting and also to make a total ass out of myself."

*　　*　　*　　*

Mark was wishing that he had slipped on an extra sweater or light jacket for his planned evening performance, but the scotch he had at Will's would just have to serve as his anti-freeze from the cold night air. He continued rummaging through a trash dumpster searching for a particular item. He had on Will's old fishing hat, and a yard stick was sticking out of his belt. He was having one hell of a time moving around because the protruding yardstick hit something every time he turned. His sympathy went out to the sword carriers of years gone by. He kept wondering to himself just how those cavaliers managed any kind of mobility or nobility in mixed company, especially around ladies.

His mind was attempting a silent communication with the Art Department's dumpster, "Indeed a plume…something, anything that could be used as a plume. My damn campus office for a plume!" His hand finally came across a strip of crepe paper. "Ahh," he thought, "This will have to do." He tore it into the configuration needed for his elegant hat and set out to find Adena's dormitory window. He had a slight idea of its location. He managed to walk and maneuver through the tall bushes that surrounded her dorm. As he neared what he thought would place him directly below Adena's window, he parted the bushes, and to his surprise, there stood old Mulrooney, the campus guard.

The unexpected confrontation drained just about all of the blood out of Mulrooney's aged face.

Mark addressed him in a rather loud whisper, and Mulrooney was trying to figure out who was standing in front of him. It took a few seconds, but Mulrooney finally figured out that it was Professor Phillips.

"Mulrooney?! What in the hell are you doing here?!" The same question about Professor Phillips went through the mind of Mulrooney. "And those binoculars around your neck? Aren't you a bit old for this kind of voyeurism?"

Mulrooney answered with the only thing that came to his mind, "I…I…I'm trying to protect the girls, professor."

"I think you'd better stick to the parking lot and your flashlight, Mulrooney." Mark's mind clicked into gear, and he realized that this confrontation might just work to his advantage.

"I'm going to make you a deal, Mulrooney…I won't say a word to Sgt. Powers about our little run-in this evening if you don't answer calls of assistance from this dorm for about the next hour. A deal?"

Mulrooney pondered the deal for a quick half-second and then extended his bony and wrinkled hand, "You got a deal." He gave Mark a brief, almost toothless smile and quickly disappeared in the brush.

Mark figured that about two more clumps of bushes and he should be directly under Adena's window. He was having a very difficult time maneuvering through the bushes. Not only was the sword a pain in his posterior, but Will's old fishing hat was catching itself on every branch. Finally, concluding in his mind that he was in the right location, he stepped out of the bushes and into the clearing. He bent over and picked up a few pebbles off the ground, and as gently as he could, tossed them against what he hoped would be Adena's window. With each toss of a pebble, he would call out her name. He breathed a great sigh of relief when Adena opened the window and looked out.

Adena was smiling from ear to ear, "Mark?! What in the world?! What are you doing here?"

"I have come to romance and **woo** my lady."

Adena's smile turned into laughter, "Professor Phillips, I do believe you've had a few too many scotch and sodas."

Mark figured that this would be an opportune moment to go into his dramatic performance.

"If you let fall upon me another harsh word

Out of that height—you'll crush me! I shall attempt quotes, a little impromptu, and a bit of paraphrasing. Bear with me…Are you ready?"

Adena raised her window as high as it would go and prepared for one of the most wonderful events of her life. She was so enthralled and so in love with the man below that tears of happiness filled her eyes.

"My dear knight, my very existence depends upon your words."

Mark, as the actor, tried to make the scene as serious as the situation would allow. He moved a few more steps toward her dorm and positioned himself directly below her window. He placed one hand on his yardstick, removed his hat, and swept it in a motion across his waist and bowed. He replaced the hat and began.

"Love, I love beyond

Breath, beyond reason, beyond love's own power

Of loving! Your name is like a violin

Its strings, the very sinews of my being

And when it starts to play I think of you,

I tremble and the strings vibrate

with—"Adena! Adena!"

My veins pulsate with, "Adena!"

Other windows of the dormitory started to open, and the girls moved into various positions within their window openings. Some listened in total disbelief; others were absorbing the romantic scene taking place right in front of their eyes.

"Is it crazy that I liken you to the sun?

That whenever I look upon you for any

length of time

I am blinded by your beauty.

The warmth of your presence, your closeness

Revitalizes in me the very atoms of spring

I thought were lost for the rest of my
    eternity."

Adena blew him a kiss, "That was beautiful, Mark!" With that comment of endearment coupled with Professor Phillips' performance, it wouldn't be long before the entire campus would know about this event.

Mark immediately took a cue from Adena's kiss.

"A kiss, one kiss. And what is a kiss
    once given?
A contract sealed—a vow
Taken before an altar of memories—
A brand of the given—a touch frozen
In time and space—A bond murmured
To beckoning lips apart—a wrap of time made
Eternal, with a parade of unseen wings—
A baptism of soft petals, a new song
Sung by an old and young heart to an ancient
    tune—
A Saturn ring, a universal ring around
    two souls
Together, forever, alone!"

An interfering noise came from one of the windows, and all of the girls, practically in unison, shouted out, "Be quiet!"

Mark didn't skip a beat.

"Your warmth and radiance is confusing
    the magnolias
They imagine it's spring and are beginning
    to bloom
Even the roosters are confused and yonder
Hens
Are laying before their time.
Your light has awakened the
    campus guard"

Mark had a silent chuckle on that line.

"He is confused as is my heart.
He thinks he has slept the night away.
O! Fortunate mortal to witness beauty
    sublime
My age, for just an instant

Has been halted in search
   of time."
Mark started to move back into the bushes.
"Adieu, my beloved, until the morrow."

*   *   *   *

Aside from the excitement Adena was bringing into his life, a phone call from his daughter, Salina, keeping him posted as to her whereabouts in the Americas, would add to his blood pressure. He received a call from her a few days following his dramatic debut under Adena's dormitory window.

"Dad, can you still hear me? This connection is lousy."

"Did you hear all of my acting story?"

"Yes, Dad, I heard it all. It's so wonderful to hear you laugh. I mean, hell, you were the talk of campus before I left. Your association, or should I say affair, with Susan was the main topic of conversation." Salina started to laugh into the phone, "So, you are now known as Professor Cyrano...I'm so glad that you're happy, Dad. Adena must be super."

"Where are you and Barry now?"

"We're in a beautiful little town called Golfito in Costa Rica. We anchored out in the Bay of Golfo Dulce. We're not too far from shore, so we just dingy in whenever something is needed or when we want to do a little sightseeing. It is, in spots, quite a romantic place. You and Adena should be here. The mountains in the distance really add to its charm. The people are called Ticos, and they're the most friendly of all we have met, so far. We will be leaving tomorrow and will sail up the western coast of Central America. Somewhere along the coast, Barry wants to veer off for Australia."

Every phone call reminded Mark of how much he missed his daughter.

"Take care of yourself. Needless to say, I love you. You're in my thoughts every day. I'm sure the feeling has come across with every phone call, I still worry like hell...Please give me a call before you brave the Pacific."

"I promise, Dad. Give my love to Adena, and tell her that I can't wait to meet her."

CHAPTER 8

▼

"To love someone deeply gives you strength
Being loved by someone deeply gives you courage."

—Lao Tzu

A young lady, a sophomore resident working at her part-time job, was busy behind the registration desk of Adena's dormitory. The lobby was quite large, but a major portion of it served as a lounge and television area, making the reception space very small. The curved stairway ascending from the lobby could have been plucked out of any old Southern antebellum plantation mansion. A young teenaged boy entered the lobby and crossed to the desk carrying a very large, cumbersome cardboard carton and a fancy, decorated corsage box.

"Excuse me," the boy said as he approached the desk.

The young lady had her back to the front entryway and was sorting and putting up the dormitory mail. She turned and faced the young man.

"Can I help you?"

"You sure can. I have a delivery for Miss Adena Rutherford."

"I'll take it. I'll leave a note in Adena's box and post a notice on her telephone that we have a delivery for her in the office. Do I have to sign anything?"

"No, ma' am…" The boy handed her the two boxes. He then pulled a letter out of his jacket pocket. "This letter goes with the two packages. It's very important that she receive this with the packages." The girl at the desk assured the young man that everything would be given to Miss Rutherford at the same time. She thanked him for making the delivery; however, she wished he hadn't used the expression 'ma' am'. For some reason, it made her feel old.

Later that evening, Mark entered the lobby exactly at nine o'clock. As he approached the stairway, Adena descended in a beautiful yellow and gold antebellum gown. She was also wearing a gorgeous corsage that complimented her attire. Her hair was done up in a crown. A wide purple ribbon circled the crown and dropped down onto her shoulders. To Mark, she was absolutely stunning! Mark was meeting her in a well-tailored Yankee officer's uniform. His boots shone like they were made from patent leather. Once again, he was wearing a sword, but this time it was real and fitted into a scabbard. He had his gloves tucked under his arm. At the top of the stairs, crammed together and looking down over the balcony railing, were at least a hundred girls, all wanting to get a glimpse of another dramatic, romantic scene executed by none other than their favorite Professor Phillips.

Looking up at Adena standing halfway down the stairway and overcoming his bedazzlement, Mark managed to speak the first words of the evening, "You, my dear, Adena, are too beautiful. No poet could find the proper words to describe you."

"And you, sir, look mighty handsome. However, I am a bit surprised to see a Yankee uniform."

Mark approached the stairs to help Adena with her final descent, "I was born in Vermont. What do you expect?" he said with a smile.

"I tried to follow your note to the letter."

"You outdid the letter's instructions!"

"Where did you get these magnificent outfits?"

"Compliments of the drama department."

"This evening's event has been on my mind the entire day. Where are we going? The campus calendar has nothing special scheduled for the entire week, and I know we aren't going to Atlanta in these outfits. Might we be going to some private ball?"

"Ask me no questions, and I'll tell you no lies. Your arm, madam." Adena grabbed his arm, and they made their grand exit from the dormitory lobby. Behind them, a hundred females sighed.

Adena had to be assisted entering Mark's little Falcon. However, they managed to overcome the obstacles. Needless to say, the sword proved a problem for Mark, so the best solution was to remove it when he was driving. As they drove across campus, Adena speculated, "If I'm not mistaken, we are heading in the direction of the Field House. Am I correct?"

"You are right on."

"What is at the gym, especially at this time of the evening?"

"A little surprise."

They had fewer problems getting out of the car than getting in. Mark led her to the front door of the field house, and a young student named Stanley opened the door on the first knock. He was dressed in a fancy waiter's costume.

"Adena, this is Stan, our personal servant, valet, and technician for this evening."

Mark escorted Adena into and onto the gym floor. The entire gym was dark except for a small, candle-lit table at center court. A huge stereo system was on the fifth row of bleachers. Stan crossed to the table, and Mark and Adena followed. As they neared the table, Stan popped the cork on a bottle of champagne and began to fill two glasses. Mark attempted to soften everything that Adena was being exposed to. "Don't be frightened by any of this. The basketball coach is a very good friend of mine and helped me arrange this event. The young man here is a very talented technical student in the Department of Drama and a personal friend." Adena moved closer to Mark and whispered in his ear, "I am the luckiest woman in the world because I have, as my lover, one of the most unique men on Earth."

"Thank you…Tonight, no rock and roll, my beloved. Since there is no decent club in this small town, except the Holiday Inn, I have taken the liberty of creating our own—with, of course, the help of Stan."

Mark handed Adena her glass of champagne. "A toast to the most beautiful Belle in all of Dixie!" They drank. "I have asked Stan to start us off with my favorite of all classical favorites, one I have always dreamed of dancing to. It is a selection that, if I could have composed it, it would have been composed especially for you…Do you know how to waltz?"

"No, but I'm a fast learner." She and Mark moved away from the table. Once again, he held her in a Mark Phillips' dancing embrace as Stan began the music with Rachmaninoff's *Symphony No. 2 in E Minor: Adagio*. Adena and Mark began to dance. Some two-step, some waltz, but within a few minutes of time, they moved across the gym floor like skaters on ice and looked as though they had been dancing together since dance was created.

Mark bent down and whispered in her ear, "I wish we could be trapped in time and that this evening could last until the end of never, but I'll tell you a fact, my dear, it will be captured in my soul forever."

They danced the night away.

*   *   *   *

The first semester was almost over. Father Time had paid heed to no man. Christmas was on the minds of all the students, along with final exams. Mark knew that any free time was drawing to a close, so he planned one more event, only this time, he had to take Adena to Atlanta, to a place that had become very special for both of them, their favorite Italian restaurant.

They were sitting at the same table as on their first visit. Candlelight provided the only illumination, and the Italian accordion player providing the romantic music, once again, approached Mark and Adena's table. Mark reached across the table and took Adena's hand. "All of this is not coincidental. I requested it about a week ago."

Adena replied, "Do you think I'm surprised?" They both laughed.

"So, how did you like the movie?"

"Well, you know how much I love the Fox Theatre. The movie enhanced the environment and definitely put me in the holiday mood. *White Christmas* does that for most people."

The Italian singer was at their table, singing a very pertinent song that fit into the ensuing scene, "That's Amore." As the singer began his selection, Mark reached into his shirt pocket, pulled out a small box, and placed it into Adena's hand. "This is a very special Christmas gift. In that small box is my heart." Adena started to unwrap it. She was shaking so much she could hardly get the paper off the little box. Once she opened it, all she could do was gasp.

"What that brilliant stone is saying is, 'Would you marry me?' You should know that I love you deeply, and I'm hoping that the feeling is mutual."

"I love you, too, Mark Phillips, with all my heart and soul. I couldn't explain to anyone the why, I just know that I love you…I accept your request."

Mark jumped up from the table, kissed the Italian singer on the cheek, and grabbed Adena and kissed her, but not on the cheek. It took another rendition of "That's Amore" before they finally broke loose from their kiss.

*   *   *   *

Two weeks had passed since Adena had slipped Mark's ring on her finger. Final exams had been taken and end-of-term papers submitted. The fall semester was now an afterthought. Everyone's mind was on the approaching Christmas vacation, shopping and partying.

Another "Goodbye Party" was going full throttle. The students had outdone themselves with the Christmas decorations, window treatments, and food preparation. The dance area was a bit shaky due to a weak floor, and the main heater left a lot to be desired. However, between dancing, eating, and drinking, no one really cared. Mark always wondered how homeowners, especially those that rented out to students, could allow their homes to become so rundown and so dilapidated.

Mark and Adena were on the dance floor, dancing to the music of "I'm Dreaming of a White Christmas." The song ended, and Mark asked Adena to pardon him for a moment so that he could refill his glass with some more Christmas cheer.

"While I'm in the kitchen, can I get you anything?"

"A cold coke would be fine."

Another selection, "I'll Be Home for Christmas," came up on the stereo, and as it began to play, a tall, good-looking, black male entered the room and walked towards Adena. He had just finished making a few pot sales on the front porch and was heading toward the kitchen with the intent of making a few more. However, when he spotted Adena standing alone, he got the urge to dance.

He approached Adena's side, "How about a dance? You look lonely."

"No thank you...I'm waiting..."

The young black man didn't wait for Adena's answer, he just grabbed her and started to dance. As he started to move, Mark's hand came down on the boy's shoulder with such a thud, that the floor shook and the record on the stereo went into reject. Mark pulled him away from Adena. Adena was a bit shocked because she had never seen Mark act this way or speak in such a heated and raspy tone.

"Get the hell away from her, Jarvis! I don't know who invited you to this party, but I'm telling you to leave before I call a few of my friends in blue uniforms."

Adena was trying her best to understand Mark's violent reaction. The young man whom Mark referred to as "Jarvis" responded to Mark's order.

"Okay, okay, Mr. Mark. Don't blow your cool. I was just trying to enjoy a little of the Christmas spirit. I didn't know you were going to be at this carnival. See ya around." As he moved toward the front door, he passed close to Mark's ear and whispered, "Still sweatin' about Regina, huh, Honkey?"

Mark took a swing at his chin but missed as Jarvis ducked and made a swift run to the door.

Adena rushed to Mark's side.

"What in the hell is going on?! This Jarvis character, who is he?"

"The son-of-a-bitch that controls Regina!"

*   *   *   *

Mark had a literary meeting scheduled for Georgia Southern College, in Statesboro, Georgia, a week before Christmas; consequently, he jumped at the opportunity to take Adena to her home in Albany. On their way south, they could stop in Atlanta, do a little Christmas shopping, and take in supper at their favorite Italian restaurant.

While stopping overnight in Macon, both had agreed that it would be proper to remove Mark's engagement ring until Adena had the opportunity to talk to her parents about their engagement. Adena felt that the shock of seeing the ring on her finger would put the pre-Christmas cheer into the sleigh of the Grinch. Mark was totally sympathetic.

Mark pulled his overly packed Falcon into the driveway of Adena's home. Adena's mother had been expecting them to arrive at any time. She was keeping guard through the front curtains when they pulled in. Mark got out of the car, followed by Adena, and they removed her packages and luggage from the vehicle. On their drive down from Macon, they had both agreed that when they arrived at her house, they would not show any physical signs of affection.

As Adena looked at the front of the house and saw her mother peeping through the front window curtains, she could have told Mark that her mother would react violently to their engagement. Her mother's reactions would center on their age differences and most certainly on Mark's position as a low-paid professor, a person with no wealth and very few, if any, investments. Adena knew that the path ahead was going to be difficult and very negative.

"Thank you for driving me home, Mark. I'll drop the bomb about our engagement right after Christmas. I know that it will have catastrophic consequences."

Mark helped Adena carry her luggage and boxes of wrapped Christmas presents to the front door.

"Wait for me just a few minutes, and you can drop me by the newspaper office on your way out of town."

"I'll wait," he said with a reassuring smile.

Carrying as much luggage as she could handle Adena rushed into the house and deposited it quickly in the hallway. She gave a quick hug to her step-father and yelled out to her mother that she was home, knowing all too well that her mother already knew. In the meantime, Carl, her stepfather, helped her with a few of her packages, went to the front door, closed it behind him, and began a conversation with Mark.

"Hello, Professor Phillips."

"Hello again, Mr. Getz, and Merry Christmas to you."

"Same to you Professor, and thank you for bringing Adena home." Carl lowered his voice and took a few steps toward Mark.

"Professor, I'd like to ask you a very personal favor."

"Go right ahead," said Mark.

"My wife and I would like to have a private chat with you after you drop Adena off at the newspaper office. I am assuming that is where she is going. They called the house and requested that she show up for work as soon as possible. And I would appreciate it if you wouldn't mention anything about this request to Adena."

Mark immediately sensed that some kind of trouble was in the works. He would keep quiet until after the meeting and call Adena as soon as he arrived in Statesboro, or maybe even sooner, depending on the subject and outcome of the "private chat."

"You have my word, Mr. Getz."

"Thank you. We will expect you in about thirty minutes."

*   *   *   *

Thirty minutes after dropping Adena off at the newspaper office, Mark found himself sitting in the Rutherford/Getz kitchen. Carl was at the stove pouring coffee, Mark was sitting at the kitchen table, and Adena's mother was standing.

Carl poured a cup of coffee for Mark, "Do you take sugar or cream?" Mark noticed that Carl was a bit nervous because the coffee cup and saucer he was holding were shaking.

"Just black, thank you."

Carl crossed from the kitchen counter to Mark and handed him his coffee.

"Mr. Phillips, I'm a man of few words..." Carl took a nervous glance at Adena's mother, "...So if you don't mind, I'll get right to the point."

"Go right ahead, Mr. Getz." Mark knew that whatever the topic, it was going to be coming at him, now.

"My wife and I have been getting some torrid stories and reports out of Magnolia about some of your antics with our daughter. Needless to say, we have not found them very amusing." There was a very long pause. Carl cleared his throat and continued, "Are you and Adena having an affair?"

Mark knew that the shot at Fort Sumter had been fired. He knew that Adena was in for it as soon as she returned from her Christmas job, so he figured that he would get in a volley of his own. "As a matter of fact, Mr. and Mrs. Getz, not only are we having an affair, but we have become engaged to be married." He said it as slowly and as softly as he could. Mrs. Getz's mouth fell open, and Carl dropped his cup of coffee.

*   *   *   *

Snow in southern Georgia in December was a rarity; however, rain was always ready to take its place. The rain was falling in torrents as Mark left Albany, Georgia, and headed to Statesboro. It was the kind of rain that required motorists to stop along the side of the road. It certainly was wet for Mark, for every time he had to stop, he tried to call Adena. He wanted to contact her at her office, to reach her before she walked into what was waiting for her at home. Finally, at a little diner, about fifty miles outside of Statesboro, he made contact. He had been on the pay phone for about ten minutes and was shoveling in more coins to continue.

"Sweetheart, I am, basically, an honorable man, and I'm certainly not a liar. They were standing over me like a couple of judges on the Prague High Court of Justice. I had no alternative but to tell them the truth. I felt that doing so would lessen the onslaught that you would have to face when you walked into the house."

"You are absolutely correct," said Adena, "In fact, when I get home, it's going to be more like the Fourth of July than Christmas. I hope and pray that I can take it. Well, I don't have to hide your ring any longer." She reached in her pocket and put it on. "I'm going to be holding it and touching it quite a bit within the next few hours."

"Will you forgive me?" said Mark.

"Only if you make me a promise to come to my rescue, if necessary."

"You just call me, and I will put my little Ford to its ultimate speed test. It will feel like it just entered the Indy 500." Adena managed a weak laugh on the other end of the line.

*   *   *   *

When Adena pulled into her driveway, she made a quick check to be sure that she still had Mark's numbers where he could be reached in Statesboro. She had a definite feeling that she would be needing them before the evening was out.

When she entered the house, she went straight to her bedroom. A minute passed, maybe less than a minute, before her mother was knocking on the door. Her mother did her best to control her emotions, but it didn't take very long before her true self came to the surface.

"You…you have disgraced this family, Adena!" Her tone became more erratic as she continued, "The talk circulating about you and your professor friend preceded your visit home by about three weeks!"

"I'm truly sorry, mother. I wanted to confide in you, but something told me that it would be useless."

"Sorry!?…Sorry?…" She had missed altogether Adena's closing sentence. "…for making yourself into a little tramp? Prostituting your body for a two-bit professor who is twice your age!"

Adena was doing her best to hold back her anger and disgust at her mother's words. "What does age have to do with it? There's almost twenty years difference between you and Carl!"

"When we married, we had already lived a major portion of our lives! You're just beginning yours…I thought I had raised an intelligent, wise daughter. Instead, you have turned into…into…a retarded harlot!" Adena thought at one point that her mother was actually going to slap her.

"I love him Mother!" At that point, Adena stood up from the bed she had been sitting on, no longer able to fully control the emotions running through her body.

"Love…" Her mother was almost shouting. "What in the hell do you know about love?!"

Adena's anger dissipated, and now, looking at her mother standing next to her bed in a fit of rage, actually felt sorry for her.

"And what do you know of love, Mother? You have never experienced it in your life!"

Though it was Adena's bedroom, her mother shouted for her to get out. "Get out of my sight!…Your sight…your tongue and presence are turning my stomach!"

Adena ran out of her bedroom and into the den. She knew that her 'family' Christmas was over. The damage was too deep. She was just about ready to call Mark when her younger sister, Sheryl, ran into the room screaming, "What have you done to our family?! Especially at Christmas time?!…I hate you…I hate you…From this day forward, I have no sister named Adena!" She ran out of the den.

Tears started to pour down Adena's face. Sheryl broke her control and her reserve. She began to tremble. Once again, she attempted to make a phone call to Mark. As she lifted the receiver to dial, Carl entered the room, rushed to the phone, and grabbed the receiver out of her hand.

"Who are you calling?"

Adena crumbled to the floor and, barely audible, called out to Mark, "Mark...I need you...I love you."

*   *   *   *

Early the next morning, the rain had left behind a beautiful sunrise. Mark didn't even have the opportunity to unpack a bag in Statesboro before receiving a phone call from Adena asking him to return to Albany right away. From the time of his departure from Albany and his arrival in Statesboro, Mark had captured very little sleep and his body was reminding him of that when he pulled into the driveway of Adena's home. He was near exhaustion.

No sooner had he stepped out of the car than Adena was in his arms.

"I thought you'd never get here!"

Mark just held her in his arms for a few moments. He wished he could give her some of his strength, but he didn't have much to spare. For the moment, his presence gave her the courage to face the hours ahead.

With her head buried in his chest, she gave him a warning, "Be careful, Mark. My parents are ready for blood. Yours, in particular. My mother called my Uncle Thomas to come over. He's a big man. Used to play football for Georgia Tech, so be very careful."

"Don't worry about me. I'll be all right. Just worry about yourself and getting what you need to take back to Magnolia."

"Everything I need is sitting in front of the door."

As they started crossing to Adena's luggage, Uncle Thomas and Carl walked out the front door. Adena was correct; Uncle Thomas was a big man. From Mark's assessment, he weighed about three hundred pounds and stood at least a foot taller than Mark. Mark had seen bigger men during his days of football with the Marine Corps, and they hadn't given him too much trouble. Of course, that was years ago. Mark was also aware that now good old Uncle Thomas could probably knock him over with a sneeze. Uncle Thomas was the first to speak out as he and Adena approached her luggage.

"Hey, Mister Professor, I hate to tell ya, but you were not invited to set foot on this property."

Adena showed no fear of her uncle, "I called him, Uncle Thomas. He came at my request."

"But not ours!" replied Uncle Thomas. "Carl, watch this luggage. I'm going in the house to call the cops."

Adena's mother was watching the entire scene from inside the house.

Carl said, "Be reasonable, Professor Phillips. Get in your damn car and head back to where you belong! Can't you see what you're doing to this family?"

Adena crossed to one of her suitcases and picked it up in front of her stepfather. "It's not what he's doing to this family, but what all of you are doing!" She turned with her suitcase and headed toward Mark's car. Her mother came out of the house and screamed at her as she was walking away.

"Adena, this is the last time I'm telling you. Get your luggage back inside this house immediately!"

Mark saw that he had access to two more of Adena's suitcases. He grabbed them and hastily took them to the car. In the meantime, Uncle Thomas positioned himself in front of two more suitcases and packages of wrapped Christmas presents. Police sirens could be heard in the distance.

As Uncle Thomas stepped in front of what was left of Adena's belongings, he tossed down the verbal gauntlet to Mark, "You'll have to step over me, Mister, if you intend to pick up the rest of this luggage."

Adena was becoming frantic, "Uncle Thomas!"

Mark gently put his hand on her shoulder, "Calm down, Adena. Everything is going to be okay. I hope that these fellows coming down the street can level a few things out."

Two patrol cars pulled in front of the house. One parked directly beside Mark's car and the other on the street. The policemen got out of their vehicles. One crossed to Thomas, and the other crossed and stood near Mark and Adena. The officer in front of Thomas was the first to question the situation. "Okay, what's going on here?"

Thomas pointed to Mark, "That person is trespassing on private property. He is also disturbing the peace and disrupting this family." The policeman turned and addressed Mark, "Is that true, sir?...What the gentleman said about trespassing?"

Adena came to Mark's rescue, "It is not true! I invited him to this house. This was my home until last night!"

The policeman that had positioned himself near to Mark and Adena crossed over to Mark's car and began to check it out.

The policeman in front of Adena asked her another question, "How old are you, young lady?"

"I'm twenty years old," replied Adena.

The cop reached out his hand, "May I see your driver's license?" Adena reached into her purse, retrieved her license, and handed it to the officer. The officer glanced at it and walked back to the family. As he did so, the officer checking Mark's car approached Mark and spoke, "Sir, if you don't mind…just to calm things down around here…just move your car out onto the public street. We will try to iron out the problems." Mark squeezed Adena's hand and did what the officer had requested. Meanwhile, the officer approaching the family directed his comments at Adena's mother, "Is that your daughter, ma' am?"

"Not any more," was her reply.

The officer turned his attention to the big man standing by his side, "No laws have been broken around here, sir. The young lady is of legal age. I'm not going into why she invited him here, but as it is the Christmas season, my best advice is for all of you to calm down. Also, I suggest that you let the girl and her male friend pick up this luggage, providing it belongs to the young lady." The policeman, along with Adena, beckoned Mark back into the yard, and Adena told Mark that they could remove the rest of her belongings. In fact, the cop helped them carry a few items to Mark's car.

Adena was the first one to get into the car. Before Mark entered, he walked around to the cop who had given them a hand and thanked him for his assistance. As he opened his car door, he looked back at the officer and wished him and his partner a Merry Christmas.

CHAPTER 9

▼

Kindness in words creates confidence.
Kindness in thinking creates profoundness.
Kindness in giving creates love.

—Lao Tzu

Two days remained before Christmas Day. Magnolia, the night before, had picked up a dusting of snow. It didn't stick, but the thrill of seeing snow picked up everyone's holiday spirits, except Adena's. She was still feeling let down and despondent. However, she was keeping herself busy, cooking, and making ornaments for her and Mark's Christmas tree.

At her home in Albany, Georgia, her mother was making other plans, and they were not associated with Christmas. She was in the den making a phone call to Adena's biological father.

"Hello?…I would like to speak to Mr. Paul Rutherford…Yes, and please tell him that Claire is calling…Hello, Paul?…Yes it certainly is…I'm fine, thank you. And Merry Christmas to you…I'm calling for a long overdue favor…Yes, darling…You do remember your promise during our divorce trial concerning my silence about your little tax transgressions? Yes, dear, it is payback time…Well, I won't go into all the details, at the moment, but there is a certain professor at North Georgia State University…Yes, dear, our Alma Mater."

*   *   *   *

Mark and Adena were nestled in front of their Christmas tree. They had taken a quick trip out to Mark's land, and Adena, after searching the forest area for nearly an hour, selected a scraggly, little Georgia Yellow Pine. She told Mark that she felt sorry for it, and she knew beyond a doubt that they could give it a good home for the holidays. The tree was directly in front of them, decorating Mark's small front room. Mark had helped her trim the tree with strings of popcorn and cranberries. The weight of the cranberry strings made the limbs of the little tree stick straight out from the trunk, but aside from that little disfigurement, the little tree was holding its own. Adena had cut up some thin strips of aluminum foil and used them as tinsel. At the top of the tree was an aluminum star that would have made any decorated Georgia Yellow Pine proud.

"What do you think about my quick little decorations?" asked Adena.

"Your creativity and our joint effort at decorating have changed our little toad tree into a Christmas prince!" Adena snuggled close to Mark. Christmas music was coming from the stereo.

"Hold me tight...I feel a bit lost...Like it's you and me against a very bitter and cruel world."

"I understand. However, over a period of time, I sincerely believe that the love we share will see us through whatever lies ahead." He lifted up Adena's face and kissed her.

"It's going to be my first Christmas away from my family. My pain is running deep." And with that comment, she wept. All Mark could do was hold her tighter in his arms.

✲   ✲   ✲   ✲

Christmas Eve had finally arrived. Mark was standing by the front door of his apartment and looking back toward the bedroom. "Are you ready?"

Adena entered the front room and took a spin in front of the bedroom door, "How do I look?"

"As beautiful as a Vermont snowflake."

"I've never seen one, but I'll take your word for it."

"Let me put it this way, every snow flake is different and unique, and that fits you to a T."

"This will be the second time in my life that I have ventured into a Catholic church. Once with my high school friend, about five years ago, and now with you, Mr. Mark Phillips...Do you think anyone will know I'm a Methodist?"

Mark started to laugh. "Only if you sing with gusto!...Tonight will be my last midnight Mass. We will be married by this time next year, and I will no longer be a Catholic. I'll explain all that later, which means that next year I will be going to the Methodist church with you, so I will need to practice my singing, especially my gusto!" He took a few steps from the front door and started singing to Adena,

"Someday..." He gestured for her to join him, and she did.

"Somewhere..." They both smiled as Mark took her into his arms.

"Somehow…"

Adena ended the duet with, "We'll have a lifetime together."

Mark grabbed her up into his arms and carried her across the front room floor to the front door, lowered her to the floor, and spoke another line of the song as he took her by the hand and down the stairs. "Take my hand and we're halfway there!"

As they were heading down the road in Mark's little Falcon toward the Catholic church, Adena made a special appeal to Mark, "Sweetheart? Will you do something special for me, and for someone else that loves you?"

"On this special evening, your wish is my command."

"Stop by and pick up Regina. If you don't know where she lives, I do. Let's take her to church with us."

There was a long pause, but Mark finally responded, "If that will make you happy."

"It will make me very happy. And, because you love her deeply, it will make you very happy."

Later that evening, as the Mass progressed, Mark found himself feeling like the luckiest person in the world. Before leaving for Mass, he had heard from Salina and Theresa, both wishing him a Merry Christmas, and both talked to Adena for the first time. Also, Adena had received a long phone call from her oldest sister. There were a few spells of crying but mostly tears of happiness. And now, here he was, enjoying his last Christmas Eve Mass, with a woman on either side of him that loved him deeply. What more could a man ask for? He held their hands throughout the Mass, and as he thought about the past and future, his eyes became misty with joy. Mass ended, as it usually did, with the singing of "Oh Come, All Ye Faithful."

On the way home, Adena cuddled up close to Mark. Regina was in the back seat.

"Thanks, Dad, for coming to pick me up tonight. It's probably the best Christmas present of my life. I needed to be reminded of where I came from and where I want to go. I'm surprised that the roof didn't cave in when I walked into Saint Luke's. Even Father Leahy recognized me!"

"I haven't held your hand in church for a long, long time. It was wonderful that you joined us. And I must say that you need to thank Adena for the idea, and I am thanking her…" Mark gently squeezed Adena's hand, "…for making this Christmas Eve a night to remember."

As Regina was leaving the car, Mark asked her one last question, "When is your reporting date for the Army?"

"In three weeks."

Overjoyed that there was no "if" in her answer, he continued, "Will you be departing from here?"

"Yes, sir. I'll be leaving for basic training via the good old Magnolia Greyhound Bus Station…Will you come to see me off?"

"I'll be there. A horde of Cyclops couldn't hold me back."

Regina opened the front door of the car and leaned across Adena to reach her father and kissed him on the cheek. "Thanks, Dad, and I love you." As she withdrew from the car, she also thanked Adena for one of the best Christmas Eves ever. She shut the car door and disappeared into the night. Adena gave Mark a big hug as he pulled away from the sidewalk.

*   *   *   *

Four days before New Year's Eve, at three a.m., a phone rang in the bedroom of Dr. Harry Smith, Dean of Humanities, NGSU. The dean and his wife were sound asleep until the phone pierced into their dreams. The dean rolled over towards his nightstand and picked up the receiver. "Hello?"

"This is Dave."

"Who is it, honey?" asked the dean's wife as she rolled over to face the lamp that her husband had just turned on.

"It's Dave."

"Dave who?"

"President of the University."

"At this time of the morning?" The dean's wife sat straight up in bed. "Is the campus on fire or what?"

The dean tried to share the phone with his wife as the president was speaking.

"…Sorry to bother you at this hour of the morning, Harry, but I've been on the phone for the past hour with some ranting German/American. He said that he'd been trying to get in touch with me for the past week. As you know, I've been away enjoying Christmas vacation. Anyway, the whole conversation was about Mark Phillips."

"Mark Phillips?" replied the dean.

"Yes, Mark Phillips, English Department. It seems, according to this man's charges, that Mark has seduced his step-daughter, a Miss Adena Rutherford. He wanted to know if we realize how perverted Mark is and said that we need to hold a housecleaning to rid our faculty of sexual deviates and perverts that deceive and destroy the morals of our innocent young female students. I realize that we are still in the holiday period—knowing Mark Phillips, I think this whole thing reeks and that Mark is innocent of all charges—however, you need to get Mark on the carpet as soon as possible and find out just what in the hell is going on."

The dean was stunned by the information dealing with one of his favorite faculty members. He could remember, just before the holidays, a report of Mark pulling some kind of dramatic stunt outside the girl's dormitory, but that was it.

"Yes, sir. I'll get on it first thing this morning."

The dean's wife was fully awake and wanted to know exactly what was going on that required a phone call before dawn.

"It's Mark Phillips…he's finally romanced himself into a cauldron of burning oil."

The dean's wife simply shook her head and replied, "Ohh, no. Poor Mark."

Mid-morning of the next day, Adena and Mark pulled up in front of the dean's home. Dean Smith was busy raking up stacks and stacks of pine needles. When he saw them drive up, he dropped his rake and beckoned them over to the front door.

"Good morning, Mark." The dean gestured out to his piles of pine needles, "Need any pine straw?"

"No, thanks, Harry."

The dean looked over Mark's shoulder, "I'm assuming that this radiant-looking young lady is Adena?"

"You are correct. Adena, I would like you to meet Dean Smith."

Adena walked forward and shook the dean's hand. Following the formalities, the dean ushered them into his home and into the study. The dean seated himself behind his desk and Adena and Mark in front. They entered into a thirty-minute discussion period and were interrupted by Alice, the dean's wife, when she entered the study bringing everyone a hot morning cup of coffee. Knowing the content of the meeting, she said her hellos, met Adena, and begged them to excuse her as she had a pie baking in the oven that needed attention. The dean sipped his coffee and continued where the conversation had been interrupted, "…so all of this turmoil is a result of you two getting engaged?"

"Yes, sir. My position, my economic situation, and my age were things, apparently, that Adena's parents could not accept. And, as I have told Adena, I can certainly understand their feelings. As you know, Harry, I have three daughters of my own."

The dean moved slightly in his chair and looked sternly at Adena, "Adena…do you love this man?" He gestured in Mark's direction.

"Yes, sir." she replied without hesitation.

The dean continued, "And the man you are in love with did nothing to seduce your mind or your body?"

"He did both sir..." Both the dean and Mark bolted upright in their chairs. "But I wanted him to do it because I loved him." Adena smiled at both men.

Mark and the dean started to laugh.

"Okay, the inquisition is over." The dean was still laughing and shaking his head in front of the two in his study. "Both of you take off and enjoy the remainder of the holidays. As far as I'm concerned, neither one of you is guilty of anything but falling in love. Don't forget to invite Alice and me to the wedding." The dean escorted them both back to their car and returned to his passion of raking pine needles.

*   *   *   *

The ultra-exquisite gentlemen's club, The Velvet Lounge, on Peachtree Street, Atlanta, Georgia was bustling with the business luncheon crowd. It had a regular clientele and was the exact opposite of the Holiday Inn in Magnolia. Everyone entering the lounge was met at the front door by a valet, then a doorman, then a greeter to identify members and check membership cards. Each drink ordered, alcohol or otherwise, would cost as much as what an average man makes in four hours of labor. Pink granite and gold décor were everywhere. The only thing lacking to the interior decoration was diamonds. Beautiful carved classic statues of Greek athletes adorned the walls, and the tiled floors made it easy for any male to discover what color underwear his lady friend might be wearing on a particular day. It was here that Paul Rutherford, Adena's biological father, had arranged a meeting with a former acquaintance called Hank Bledsoe. They had already consumed enough drinks to pay for a day's service of an attorney.

Paul finally brought the conversation to the precise reason behind the called meeting,

"Hank, it appears that I have to use your services once again."

"What is it this time, Mr. Rutherford?"

"My ex-wife doesn't see money and prestige at the end of the rainbow for one of my daughters."

Hank had a stunned look on his face. "I didn't know you had children!"

"No one knows except the IRS. We all make mistakes in our lives. I made three of them because I married a beautiful, extremely sexy woman whom I had the hots to possess. I guess if you count the marriage, I made four big mistakes. Every time I fucked her, she was counting my money."

"So,..." replied Hank, "...if you hate your ex, why are you doing something for her?"

"Very simple, Hank. When we got divorced, she held back information that could have hung me with the IRS. I told her for holding back that information, I would be in her debt...I never dreamed that she would request what she has."

A nearly naked cocktail waitress who would have made Dionysus look twice came to the table with more drinks, picked up the empties, excused herself for interrupting the conversation, and quickly moved on to another table. Hank followed her every movement to the next table, shook his head, and returned his attention to Paul.

"So, what's the deal?"

"Apparently, my middle daughter, and for the life of me, I can't even remember her name, has fallen in love with one of her professors at North Georgia State University. The professor in question, a Mark Phillips, is twenty or more years older than my daughter."

Hank took another glance at the waitress as she went by, "Wow! He must like em young!"

"He is also divorced and poor. The latter worries my wife more than anything else."

"So, what does she want?"

"She wants him destroyed. Not wiped out, mind you, only destroyed."

"She ain't asking for much is she?"

"Next week, take a trip over to the University and see what kind of information you can dig up on this guy and check back with me about our possibilities."

Hank raised his drink and made a toast, "Here's to the old professor. May he enjoy it while he can!"

*   *   *   *

The Greyhound Bus station of Magnolia, Georgia, was quite a landmark. Thousands upon thousands of students had come and gone from this bus terminal. As Adena stood in the waiting room with Mark, she tried to absorb the history. She wondered if anyone ever had been interested in doing some kind of feature story or perhaps a history book about the various old Greyhound Bus terminals throughout America. What stories they could tell. Her journalistic imagination took her back to World War II and how so much sadness and joy had been experienced right in the spot she was standing. When they left, when they returned, and when they didn't. For Mark's sake, she was praying that this day would be a joyous one. She looked up at the wall clock. It was ten minutes to ten. For about the eighth time in thirty minutes, since she and Mark arrived at the station, Mark interrupted her thoughts. She had never seen him this tense and outwardly nervous.

"Her bus leaves at ten!...Where is she?...Why didn't she let us pick her up?"

"Because she didn't want anything or anybody to influence her decision...Regina wanted to do this all by herself." Adena crossed to Mark and took hold of his arm. "Calm down, Mark. We have been standing here for almost an hour, and as each minute ticks away, your tension level rises. You're going to explode before she gets here."

"You mean, if she gets here."

Adena was beginning to lose her patience, "Mark Phillips, you are beginning to lose one of those beautiful characteristics that I fell in love with. You have told me many times about your steadfast faith in man's overall ability to make 'right' decisions. Your daughter fits in there somewhere. Don't lose your faith in one short hour."

Mark's face took on a glow. It looked like someone had plugged him in and the light went on. He was looking over Adena's shoulder when he saw Regina turn the corner and head in the direction of the station. She was carrying two large suitcases, and she was about two blocks away. All Mark could do was shout, "She's coming!...Dear, God, she's coming!"

Mark glanced back at the clock on the wall. It now read two minutes to ten. As he turned back to look at his daughter, her bus pulled into the station. Both he and Adena were holding hands, and with the passing of each second, their grip got tighter and tighter.

"Adena, she stopped! And she put down her suitcases!" Adena could hear Mark in prayer, his voice was low but audible to her. "Don't turn back, baby...Don't even look back...Walk, damn you—walk to your freedom!...To your new life!..." He dropped his head onto Adena's shoulder almost sobbing, "I can't look any more. I just can't."

Adena squeezed Mark's hand and whispered Regina's movements into Mark's ear. "She looked back, Mark, but she has picked up her suitcases and is heading this way in a run!"

Mark and Adena broke hands, and both rushed outside to meet her. Tears were flowing from all three. Regina hugged Adena and asked her to watch over her father. Mark gave his daughter one last hug, and she stepped into the bus.

*   *   *   *

Dean Smith, Dean of Humanities, had never run across such a problem as he was having to deal with today, especially with one of his most favored and talented faculty members. His phone at home had been ringing all morning long, and all of the calls were from members of the State Board of Regents wanting to know what in the hell was going on at North Georgia State University. The president had given him a call as soon as he walked in his office and said that the problem had to be solved once and for all, even if it meant removing Mark and placing him on sabbatical leave until all of this blew over. Both the dean and president knew that they might be headed straight into a clash with the American Association of University Professors. The charges leveled against Mark, were simply unproven allegations. However, some action had to be taken.

"Dean Smith," came the call over the intercom, "Professor Phillips is here for his appointment."

"Send him in."

Mark entered the dean's office and walked to the dean and shook his hand.

"Well, we meet again. I apologize for being late."

"Hell, Mark, you're only eight or ten minutes behind, so don't worry about it. Have a seat."

Mark moved back around the dean's desk and pulled up a chair.

"I'm sure that you are aware of why I called you to my office."

"Yes, sir."

The dean picked up a sheet of newspaper from his desk and moved it in the direction of Mark. "Have you seen this piece of trash?"

The headlines read, "NORTH GEORGIA STATE UNIVERSITY CONDONES DEBAUCHERY WITHIN ITS FACULTY!"

"Yes, sir. And I have read it at least a hundred times since it came out in yesterday's paper."

"The president has been hounded by reporters from the Atlanta Constitution as well as television newsmen since that article hit the newsstands." The dean took a pause, looked out the window, and shook his head. "I assume that you are going to sue for slander?"

"No, sir."

The dean, with disbelief written all over his face, turned in his chair to face Mark. "Damn it, Mark, don't you realize that if you don't take that bastard to court, I'm going to have to ask for your resignation?!"

"I can't do it, sir. I will not drag a member of Adena's family through the courts. If I did, and I know I could win the case, I would be making her step-father out a fool, and I can't do that."

"And, to let it stand…you are ruining your reputation and placing a black mark against this university and the entire academic community, for that matter?"

"I'm sorry, Harry, and you know that I'm sincere when I say that."

"I realize that a king gave up his throne for a woman he loved, but in your situation…You've served this university for twelve years, Mark. You even brought us national prestige and recognition through your publications. For God's sake don't force me into letting you go." A long period of silence ensued. "What is Adena's reaction to all of this?"

"She is as abhorred and reviled by this article as I am, especially so because she is a journalism major. However, she wants me to do what I think is right under the present circumstances."

"Does she want you to take her stepfather to court over this?"

Mark shook his head in the affirmative, "She does, but in using my own judgment, I believe she has suffered enough for falling in love with me. Her youngest sister has already disowned her, and her grandparents are in a state of shock over everything that has happened within the past couple of months. I just can't do it, Harry."

"Very well, Mark. In a way, I can understand your position. I hope you can understand mine. I must tell you now that your contract will not be renewed, nor will summer employment be offered. Forgive me, Mark, but you leave me no alternative."

Mark stood and once again reached out his hand, "Thank you for your concern, Harry. And, believe me, having worked in the academic world for most of my adult life, I understand your position." Mark turned slowly and left the Dean's office. When he closed the door behind him, Dean Smith slammed his fist on the desk, stood up, and walked to the window. He watched Mark leave the building and walk to his car and thought, "What a loss…and what a compassionate individual."

*   *   *   *

Hank Bledsoe had wracked his brain for two weeks to come up with some kind of plan that could destroy a reputable, professional individual. His investigative work, spread over two weeks, brought together a few facts that he could possibly use to bring about the professor's downfall. The article written about Mark in the <u>Atlanta Constitution</u> was a start. Bledsoe had also discovered that the professor was quite a ladies' man, another possible area to pursue. The professor's contract had been terminated at NGSU, which meant that he would be sending out mail in search of other positions.

Mr. Bledsoe was the epitome of the unsavory individual that seems to thrive in human society. He lived off the suffering of others. Many unscrupulous individuals, past and present, love to make their riches off the spilled blood and agony of people. A certain glee is achieved by the "Bledsoe" type of human when others suffer because of their vile actions and decisions. Their glee is heightened when they can prosper from the suffering.

Taking the slanderous article published by the <u>Atlanta Constitution</u>, Bledsoe laid out his plan. To destroy an individual like Professor Phillips, he had to destroy his character, his confidence, and his ability to make a living. Bledsoe's first endeavor was to contact as many women as he could who had slept with Phillips. To involve them in his scheme, he had to find those women that had a debt to repay, perhaps felt jilted or treated wrongly, or simply find women that loved easy money. They were not hard to find.

The next part of his plan was to approach Mark's home mailman. Bledsoe knew that everyone had a price. How could a simple mailman turn down the offer of a new car? Once Bledsoe had this individual in his pocket, he captured the allegiance of a couple of mail clerks at the University post office. Their price was much less than the U. S. mailman's. He had to sign up a couple more individuals on the team, and they had to come from the Magnolia U. S. Post Office. Once again, people proved Bledsoe's point that everyone has their price. Once he had them, they were had. The professor's destruction was, according to Bledsoe, "In the bag."

*   *   *   *

The Garden of Eden for Mark and Adena was Mark's property. Locked away in its own seclusion, they both could find a certain peace and tranquility within the womb of the forest. It was mid-spring, and the sun was in control of the day, a perfect time for a picnic. Mark and Adena had found the area where they first attempted an outdoor picnic. They had spread out their blanket and were basking in the sun. Adena, looking straight up to the heavens, broke the silence, "It's so peaceful here...And the sun so warm." She rolled over to Mark's side and placed her arm around him. "Our wedding will be so simple and yet so beautiful! Do you want me to wear flowers in my hair?"

Mark moved sideways to face Adena, "Flowers would be wonderful. A frame of God's splendor around a radiant..." Mark paused and saw that Adena had absorbed her share of the afternoon sunshine. He had to smile when he said, "...sun kissed face."

"Mark?" She looked deep into his eyes with concern written all over her face. "Will we still be able to marry here, now that you've lost your position at the University?"

"How did I know that that was on your mind? Everything is going to transpire just the way we planned it...I'll find another position, and whether it's in Maine or California, I promise that we will be standing before a preacher..." Mark raised up and pulled a corner of the blanket back toward him revealing the earth below, and with his index finger drew a large X into the earth, "...right on top of this X come October."

Adena smiled and pulled Mark back to her, "What are your plans for this summer?"

"You're full of questions this afternoon. At the moment, I don't know. I'm sure I'll find something in this area to keep me busy through July. Bills must be paid. If things like the mail, interviews, and candidate selections go accordingly, I'll be moving to my new position around the first week in August, maybe even sooner."

"I'm looking for an apartment and a job. I checked at the local newspaper, but the summer period is their slowest season. I'll find something."

Mark moved closer and nuzzled his mouth to her ear, "You could always move in with me after they close the dorms."

Adena gently pushed him back and gave him a stern look, "Mark Phillips!...We have already discussed that possibility and we both agreed that I need to be independent for awhile and have a place of my own in case of a surprise visit from a member of my family...Which at this time seems very unlikely."

"They will come around, eventually. Believe me. Enough questions for today."

Mark dropped back down on the blanket. "Will you lower that beautiful face and kiss me?"

Adena immediately complied. The kiss was long and passionate. Adena broke the kiss and raised her head just enough for a breath's clearance between her lips and Mark's, "Mark?"

"Hmmm?"

"Let's christen our special place in the sun."

For just an instant, Mark had a shocked look on his face until Adena straddled him, unbuttoned her blouse and exposed her breasts. "It's your land isn't it? If someone shows up, just ask them to leave."

For the next hour, Mark's special Garden of Eden became a Garden of Ecstasy.

CHAPTER 10

▼

"No hotter flame hath burned Than the breast of a woman spurned."

—Sherry Blanton

The interior, unlike a classroom, was dimly lit to be the citadel of collegiate communication. Within the walls of this Pizza Inn passed some of the most unique and original ideas ever expressed by man. Words of wisdom, praise, encouragement, correction, and even love had been absorbed by the rather dark walls, lit not only by low wattage electric lamps but by candlelight. Whoever designed the outside and inside of this Pizza Inn knew exactly who his target audience would be. He knew that ideas would be discussed within, and comments and questions about exams and papers would abound. Conversations about classes, professors, and colleagues would take place. Dates and promises would be made, some kept, and some broken. There would be beer, tea, and soda pop drinkers, and even a few coffee fanatics who would bend their elbows on this hallowed ground. The various conversations would traverse the sound scale moving from loud to the boisterous, from the belligerent to the bellicose, to the soft and serene, to even the sublime. The designer also knew that he needed tables that would cater to the intellectual as well as to the lover.

An open kitchen provided an environment that assaulted the senses, especially the sense of smell. Upon entering the restaurant, one would be confronted with the smells of Italy. The first aroma would be that of freshly baked bread, followed by the combined aromas of onions, green and red peppers, sizzling pepperoni, bubbling hot tomato sauce saturated with oregano and garlic. All of these aromas would be topped off by the smell of melted mozzarella being smothered with lavish layers of parmesan and romano cheeses.

The Pizza Inn was located directly across the street from the campus of the University, easy access for the entire faculty and student body. The Pizza Hut, the Inn's only competitor, was located clear on the opposite side of town. The Hut catered to the town locals and alcoholic beverages were not part of their menu.

Adena had laid claim to one of the candle-lit booths at the Pizza Inn. It was mid-spring. Each booth was made to hold four people, two to a bench; however, in order to sit comfortably, one prayed that his partner had a very thin or non-existent posterior. For the seating of a romantic couple the small bench was ideal. Adena was having a late lunch and catching up on some of her reading assignments. She did not see Susan Wells and some of her sorority sisters enter the restaurant. Susan did not recognize Adena until she had made her order and turned to seek a table for her and her sisters. Upon spotting Adena, Susan instantly forgot her order and her entourage and crossed the restaurant floor to stand on the opposite side of Adena's booth.

"Well, if it isn't the rich bitch from Albany! I've been looking forward to a one on one meeting with you for the last five months."

Adena was a bit shocked at the greeting. She quickly lowered her book and looked directly into Susan's eyes. Adena replied with the only sentence that came into her head.

"Hello...Susan. It is, Susan? Correct?"

Susan simply ignored Adena's comments and forged into her verbal attack. "My, my, my, I've been told that money could work miracles but, up until now, I didn't believe it." Susan raced on without even catching a breath, "The last time I saw you was at a fall party. If I remember correctly, your hair was up in a bun, you wore no make-up to speak of, or that was noticeable, you had huge glasses hanging off the end of your nose, and your dress looked like it came from a local thrift store." Two of Susan's sorority sisters that had followed her to Adena's booth broke out in laughter. Susan kept on the attack, "God damn...you must have really wanted my ex. Now that you have him, how would you rate him on the fucking scale?" The girls behind Susan continued their spurts of laughter.

Adena shifted her position on the bench. She knew that Susan was the spurned one, the loser in the eternal love triangle, and at this moment she was out for revenge. She had an opportunity to artificially ease some of the hurt caused by Adena's appearance into her life and the life of Mark Phillips. Adena was aware that it had been a small miracle that she had avoided a face-to-face confrontation with Susan an entire semester. Nevertheless, the battlefield was now a reality.

Adena did her best to carefully select each word that came out of her mouth. As she began to answer Susan, the rest of Susan's sorority sisters had assembled at her booth.

"I did not intend to take Mark away from you, Susan, and I certainly did not plan to fall in love with him."

Susan let out a satanic laugh. "So, you had intended all along to move from glasses to contacts, from hair buns to flowing tresses, and tight fitting dresses, and from no make-up to make-up applications that would be the envy of Hollywood!? Don't give me that shit, Adena! That night at the party, I could see the desire for the man I was with written all over your face. I even felt strange vibrations when I shook your hand." Susan slowly and threateningly slid into the opposite bench and her sisters moved in and made a semi-circle around the booth.

Adena became a bit tense but was not frightened because other people were seated in the area, and a few faculty members had just entered the restaurant. She spoke in a soft voice, "Susan, I know, in some way, that you have been hurt by all of this, and for that I am extremely sorry. However…" Adena's muscles tightened, and she was preparing for whatever was going to take place, "…I will not apologize for falling in love with Mark."

Susan's body stiffened at the sound of Mark's name. She leaned across the small table. Adena could feel her breath as Susan spoke directly into her ear.

"I really didn't go with Mark with the intent of marrying him. He was old enough to be my father, for Christ's sake! I went with him because every girl on campus wanted him, and I had him. And do you know why he had a relationship with me? He loved to fuck, and so did I. He kept me well satisfied. He surprised me at being so adept at sex, considering his age. So what do you do for him, Miss Rich Bitch?" The plosive sound of the **b** from the word <u>bitch</u> splattered Susan's saliva against Adena's ear and cheek.

Adena bolted to her feet, and in the process of the movement bumped aside two of Susan's sisters. She turned and looked directly into Susan's eyes, "Susan, if you are looking for a physical confrontation then I'm ready to take on not only you but the shadows surrounding us. If you want to talk this out, I'm willing to do that on a civil level, and I would appreciate leaving the gutter language under the table where it belongs."

Susan slid out of the booth and stood face to face with Adena. Her sisters started to move in on Adena, but Susan lifted up her arms and held them back. "I'm not here for a fight. I've had my say, and I'm somewhat satisfied. It's a good thing that I graduate this spring because if I were here on campus next year, I'd make life miserable for you. However, with the recent headlines in the <u>Atlanta Constitution</u>, neither you nor professor Phillips are going to be very happy in the months ahead. As they say, "What goes around comes around." With those words, Susan spun and headed toward the front door. Her sisters followed right behind her. As they made their hasty exit, rushing directly behind them was the

Pizza Inn cashier yelling "HEY!…YOU ALL DIDN't PICK UP YOUR PIZZA ORDERS…AND YOU DIDN't PAY FOR YOUR PIZZAS!!"

Adena never mentioned her run in with Susan to Mark. For the remaining two months of the spring semester, she prayed that Susan would be too busy to pursue her revenge any further.

✳   ✳   ✳   ✳

Two weeks following Susan's altercation with Adena, Susan received a phone call from the Pizza Inn. It was not a call seeking restitution for the pizzas that she and her sisters had left behind two weeks earlier. It was a call from an Atlanta business man requesting a meeting with her at the Inn. The caller did not leave his name, but he did mention that he knew of her upcoming graduation and that what he had to talk to her about could mean quite a few extra dollars in her pocket, perhaps even a down payment on a new car. He had aroused Susan's curiosity. She gave a quick wave goodbye to her sorority sisters as she left the house and told them that she was going to the Pizza Inn for a meeting.

As Susan approached the front door to the Pizza Inn, she was greeted by Mr. Henry Bledsoe. Bledsoe escorted her inside and they sat down at one of the lighted tables. The Inn was empty except for the workers behind the counter.

Bledsoe was the first to speak. "Miss Wells, I will quickly come to the point of my visit and our meeting." Bledsoe entertained a thought between his comments as he took in the enchanting curves and beauty of Susan: "That professor has fantastic taste and must have a wicked, pile-driving ass in order to satisfy such a beauty!" He continued his conversation with Susan, "I represent a client in Atlanta that is anticipating taking a certain professor by the name of Mark Phillips to court. He does not want to lose his case of 'professor impropriety,' and he expects to show that the professor is sexually imbalanced and a threat to the female student body of North Georgia State University. From my discussions of recent days with students of the university, I have discovered that the professor's love life is 'general knowledge' amongst the student population. In one of my discussions, your name came into the picture as one of the professor's conquests. Was that information correct?"

Susan was hesitant in answering, but finally, in a soft voice answered, "Yes."

Henry Bledsoe smiled from ear to ear. He knew that he was on the verge of capturing one of the leading players in the love antics of Professor Mark Phillips.

Susan shifted in her chair and followed her reply with, "I have answered your question, Mr. Bledsoe, and now I'm asking one. Just what do you want of me, and what were you talking about when you mentioned over the phone that I had the opportunity of picking up a few dollars?"

Bledsoe proceeded very slowly, "My client and I need you to sign an affidavit saying that, if we take Phillips to court, you will testify against him and make a claim that he seduced you with wine and, against your will, had sex with you."

"That would be a bit difficult to do, Mr. Bledsoe. Our sexual interludes were always consensual."

An evil smirk came across Bledsoe's face. "Even if it meant that you picked up a few thousand dollars? Be smart, Miss Wells. He threw you over for some other broad and left you dangling. Here's your chance to get a little revenge."

Susan immediately knew the kind of character she was sharing a table with. She couldn't understand her negative reactions to him but he definitely repulsed and frightened her. She raised up out of her chair and started to cross toward the front door. Bledsoe reached out, grabbed her by the thigh, and stopped her. In his other hand, he was holding a roll of one hundred dollar bills and a folded sheet of paper.

"My client is willing to offer you, right now, ten thousand dollars to sign this affidavit."

Susan turned back to Bledsoe very slowly, allowing Bledsoe's hand to brush across her groin. Bledsoe very quickly moved his hand between her legs and gently pressed his fingers against her vagina. His business thoughts were escaping him, and he was about to burst through his trousers. Susan, with slight force, knocked his hand away from her, and slowly returned to the table, and sat down.

There was a long pause. "Where do you want me to sign?" Susan whispered.

Bledsoe leaned across the table, handed Susan the contract, and spoke softly into Susan's ear, "I'll toss in another thousand if you'll meet me at the Holiday Inn this evening around eight o'clock?"

CHAPTER 11

▼

"What lies behind us and what lies before us are tiny matters,
compared to what lies within us."

—Ralph Waldo Emerson

Summer was drawing near, and Mark Phillips was still without possible employment. Consequently, he decided to pay a visit to his future son-in-law's father, Tim Bremmer, the Tobacco Baron of North Georgia. Mark and Tim were the best of friends, but for various reasons, like falling in love, he hadn't been to visit Tim Bremmer since Adena came into his life.

Tim Bremmer, dollar for dollar and asset for asset, could stand right next to Adena's biological father, Rutherford. Tim had, and was still, making millions in the tobacco business. He owned practically every tobacco warehouse in North Georgia and grew some of the finest tobacco in the state. His land holdings in Magnolia and beyond numbered in the thousands of acres. In fact, at one time, Mark wondered if he owned the distant mountains. The Bremmer clan had arrived from Germany shortly after the Civil War and bought war-torn real estate at very inexpensive prices, and as the years went by, they simply added more acreage to their holdings. When tobacco became a lucrative crop, their fortunes and land holdings nearly doubled in the early 1900's.

Both Tim and Mark were sitting outside by Tim's Olympic-size pool. Everywhere Mark looked, he could see landscaping and gardening that probably cost Tim more than Mark made in a year. They were discussing Mark's dismissal from the University.

Tim apparently was getting a little heated, "Why in the hell aren't you taking the University to court?…You're a tenured professor, for Christ's sake…The burden of proof regarding that damn article in the paper rests on the University's shoulders, not yours!"

"I don't have the time, Tim. Besides, in the eyes of many people in Magnolia and the state of Georgia, I'm a dirty, treacherous old man. And nothing I could or would do is going to change their attitudes."

"Bullshit! Just give me the go signal, and I'll write a check and have you rein-stated within the next twenty-four hours!"

Mark started to laugh, "Not necessary, but thanks for the offer. I'll find another position, in another state, and leave all of these problems behind me...Adena and I need a new beginning. Too many people remember my ex, and too many people remember Regina's escapades. There are just too many neg-atives for Adena and me to overcome."

"Well, I for one, will miss the hell out of ya...I know you'll be back here off and on because a part of you will still be here. Speaking of Salina, have you heard from the kids? They worry the shit out of me. I haven't heard from them in over a week. I'm going to kick my son's ass up around his ears when he gets back here!"

"I was going to ask you the same question."

"The last time I heard from them was early last week."

"Well, you have the latest word."

"They were in Sydney, Australia, when they called. Their next stop, after a brief visit with the kangaroos, was to be Singapore."

"It's hard to believe that my daughter..."

"And my son..."

Mark beat Tim to the closing line by a beat, "Are halfway around the world!" They both laughed. Mark took the last sip of his scotch and soda.

"Well, I see that you took my advice when you called and brought along your bathing suit, so let's take a fast dip!" As Tim headed for the pool, he shouted back at Mark, "And listen, you jackass, the next time you come out here, bring Adena with you. I'm gonna have to check her out and see if you're telling me the truth!" With that comment, he disappeared into the water. Mark wasn't far behind. They both swam to the edge of the pool.

"Mark! You almost allowed me to forget what we were originally talking about before we started talking about your damn dismissal from the University. Hell, yes, you can work for me this summer, and so can Adena."

"Thanks, Tim."

"In fact, I've got some topping to do in one of my fields within the next cou-ple of weeks. Will you two be ready to start then?"

"Sounds great!"

"Good! Now that that is out of the way, I'll race you to the other end!"

"You're on!"

Tim was already on his second lap by the time Mark got to the end of the pool. Mark reached out and held on to the pool's edge. His hands felt like they were asleep. He was out of breath, totally out of energy and, for a brief moment, his world felt like a merry-go-round.

*   *   *   *

In a small park, located near Georgia Tech University, Hank Bledsoe and Paul Rutherford were meeting on a concrete and wooden slat bench. Paul Rutherford had been waiting for weeks to hear about the assignment he had given to Bledsoe. Had Bledsoe been successful or taken his money and left the country? When Bledsoe had contacted his office early this morning for the meeting this afternoon, Rutherford wanted to know something about what action had been taken against Professor Phillips. However, all he received from Bledsoe was a meeting time and place. He canceled all of his afternoon business appointments.

Paul Rutherford joined Bledsoe on the park bench and could not contain his curiosity any longer, "It's about time! What in the hell is happening to our little destroy operation?"

"Sorry I haven't been in touch with you as much as you'd like, Mr. Rutherford, but this operation took me longer than anticipated. Believe me, I have been busy."

"I'd like to remind you that you have called me once since I first gave you the assignment! On top of that, I have checked the special account that I set up for you, and the hundred thousand dollars that I deposited seems to have quickly disappeared. Would you mind explaining?"

"Well, you remember the first phone call. I told you at that time that the old professor had been fired from his job because of the article in the Constitution."

"Yes."

"Well, it took me awhile to figure out a plan, but most of my operation fell into place after I did some research. By the way, Rutherford, you have a beautiful, very attractive daughter."

"Forget my daughter. The only joy I remember from her came from the fantastic orgasm I experienced with her mother the night she was conceived. Tell me about your damn plan!"

Hank admired Rutherford. He had never met another man as cold-hearted as himself.

"Well, I figured that if he lost his job and couldn't find another—especially at his present pay scale—it would wipe him out professionally, economically, and mentally. His ex-wife doesn't give a shit about him as long as he pays child support for his youngest daughter. I think her name is Theresa. When he can't manage that, he is going to be in deep shit."

"Sounds good, but it doesn't explain the disappearance of my money."

"Some of your money went out for favors rendered…" Bledsoe saw the puzzled look appear on the face of Rutherford, so he attempted to explain. "The hiring of team players, capeche?"

"I think so," replied Rutherford. "Continue."

"I have all of his mail outlets covered, local, state, and federal…so, when he mails out a letter or letters inquiring about a job, they either don't go out, or I get the addresses and follow them up with this material." Bledsoe pulled out a few items from his coat pocket. "Number one is a copy of Getz's letter to the president of NGSU which covers about the same info he gave to the Constitution; item number two is a copy of the newspaper article headlined in the Constitution. The third little item is a document showing the names and addresses of over a dozen women our professor slept with, and all of them swear that they would go to court and testify against him regarding his debauchery."

Rutherford was quite impressed, "Hank, you're a genius!"

"Thank you, Mr. Rutherford. Now, in regards to your money…"

"Yes?" was Rutherford's instant reply.

"That list of female names you are holding cost you between five and ten thousand dollars a signature. The Susan Wells signature cost more than any of them. However, before I mentioned the possibility of the money, I thought she might have signed the list free of charge. I was quite mistaken. Our local mailman cost you the price of a new car, and…"

Rutherford abruptly cut him off. "I really don't give a shit about the money. Is the operation complete?"

"It's complete."

Rutherford gave Bledsoe a big smile. "Good. My debt to my ex-wife has finally been paid in full!"

*   *   *   *

The fraternity and sorority family at NGSU decided to start a new tradition. They pooled their finances and energy and held an end-of-semester party out by the lake. The entire campus community was invited. At one end of the lake, they had set up a portable stage, where the University jazz band was playing. Colored Oriental paper lanterns were hanging around different sections of the lake. One fraternity even fired off a few skyrockets to light up the night sky. Mark and

Adena were standing near the same spot that they first visited when Adena started her school year. Mark was holding her in his arms, and both were watching the skyrockets illuminate the heavens. Mark voiced his disbelief that another academic year was coming to a close. "And, what a year it has been. Remember our first visit to this spot?"

"I'll never forget."

"Believe it or not, that's when I started to fall in love with you."

"Well, I'll have to also confess that that was the day I started falling in love with you. We're even."

Mark turned Adena around in his arms so that he could look into her face. "You are aware that your name rhymes with Athena?"

"Yes? And?"

Mark smiled, "Nothing. Just filling the moment with a bit of trivia. But what I have to say to you now isn't trivia. It comes straight from my heart. You brought something into my life that I thought would never happen, and you also validated the thoughts and expressions of one of my favorite Lebanese poets."

"I know who you're talking about, Mister Smarty. I found his book on your desk, and I too have fallen in love with him and his ideas. Speaking about love, might you…" She paused because she really didn't know how to phrase her question. But she knew that Mark admired her candor so she let loose, "…be interested in having another child?" A long silence took hold of the scene. Adena could see the gears turning in Mark's mind, and then quite suddenly he pulled her tight against him.

"A child…a child conceived and born of love…What a beautiful child we will have." He closed his comment with a long, warm, loving kiss. To students passing in back of them, they appeared as a love statue in silhouette against the light of the lanterns and exploding skyrockets.

✳   ✳   ✳   ✳

Mark was busy at his typewriter in the front room of his apartment. Adena was in the kitchen, cooking and experimenting. "Hey!" she shouted, "…the person in the front room?"

"Yes?"

"Are you ready for another cup of coffee?"

"I'm ready!"

Adena entered from the kitchen with Mark's coffee and placed it on his desk, "Ohh, ohh, forgot your sweetener." She picked up his coffee and rushed back into the kitchen at the same time that the telephone rang on Mark's desk. Mark answered, "Hello?" His instant thought was a quick prayer that some college or university was calling him for a job, but the person on the other end of the line certainly lifted his spirits just as high. It was Regina calling from her basic training camp in South Carolina.

"Dad?...Dad?...Can you hear me?"

Mark called out excitedly to Adena in the kitchen, "It's Regina!...But, I can hardly hear her."

Adena rushed back into the front room and stood in back of Mark. She rested one hand on his shoulder and with her other hand, balanced his cup of coffee.

"Can you hear me, Dad? I've got some fantastic news to tell you...Can you hear me? I don't want you to miss a word I'm saying." An Army jet flew right over where Regina was standing and drowned out all possibility for clarity. When it passed, Mark yelled into the phone.

"Say something, anything, and I'll let you know if I hear you!"

"Dad?"

"You're finally coming across loud and clear. Just before that jet flew over, I heard the word fantastic. What's fantastic?"

"Dad, you're not going to believe this. Hold on to your hat, seat, or Adena if she's close by. I have been appointed to the preparatory school for West Point!"

Mark dropped the phone, jumped up, and grabbed Adena and spun her around. His cup of coffee went everywhere. Adena yelled out to him as he started to spin her a second time around. "Mark!...For God's sake tell me what has happened!"

Mark began to laugh, and tears of joy were streaming down his cheeks. "It's Regina on the phone!"

"I know it's Regina on the phone! Why the explosive celebration and the coffee baptism?"

He stopped spinning her and held her at arm's length, "She has received an appointment to the preparatory school for the West Point Military Academy!"

Adena moved toward Mark, started to laugh and gave him a big bear hug, "That's terrific. Great. Mark? Don't you think Regina would like to know how you feel? She's still on the phone."

Mark rushed back to the phone and picked up the receiver, "Regina...Regina, I'm so proud of you...and so is Adena. Yes, she's standing right here. In fact, I just gave her a coffee shower. Congratulations, honey! I've always told you that you were a genius. Okay darling,...take care. Yes,...yes, I'll tell Salina as soon as she calls me. Don't forget to call Theresa. I love you, too." Mark hung up the telephone and once again jumped up from his chair and picked Adena off the floor and spun her around.

"Whatever you were cooking—stop. We are going out on the town. Which means dinner at the Holiday Inn. I love you!" With the final spin, they both started laughing and tumbling to the floor.

✳   ✳   ✳   ✳

A week later, Mark was in his University office, going over the campus-delivered mail. His department chairman was standing by the file cabinet.

"Damn it, George! What's the matter? Look at them!" Mark picked up a stack of letters and dropped them back on his desk. "Rejects. Rejects. All of them."

His department chairman couldn't understand either, "I wish I could tell you what's wrong. I know that the market isn't that tight for English professors, especially with your background and accomplishments."

Here it is, almost the end of May, we're into final exams, and I haven't received one interview...Not even a warm letter."

"Did you start applying right after your...dismissal?"

"I started writing letters of application the day that I walked out of the Dean's office."

"What about your references?"

"I've checked them all. Excellent, excellent. Yours especially, George, and I thank you."

"What about the Dean? Did he say he would help?"

"Harry said that he would give me an excellent reference should anyone call his office. His letter was excellent. What about you, George? Has anyone called you or written you letters regarding my applications?"

Dr. Wessel simply shook his head in disbelief, "Nothing has come across my desk or over my phone. If something did, you would be the first to know. You already know that I think you're the best professor I've ever had on my staff."

"Thanks, George. I'm just beginning to get a bit nervous."

George crossed and bent over Mark and placed his hand on Mark's shoulder. "Stay in there, Mark. Something will come through. I know it."

"Thanks again, George. I hope you're right."

Dr. Wessel went to the office door and turned back in, "How's the book coming?"

Mark managed a slight smile, "It's over fifty percent finished."

"Great! Keep at it." Dr. Wessel left the office, and Mark turned and stared at the calendar on his office wall. Jesus, he thought, how things can change in the short period of a year!

Mark Phillips was standing in front of his Love in Literature class, and his students were putting away their notebooks, textbooks, and other writing paraphernalia as they prepared for their final examination. Mark wanted to give them a few last words. Adena was standing just outside the classroom.

"All of the reading, all of the discussions, and all of the note-taking is at an end. It is time to record some of the things that you have learned. Before you start taking your exam, I'd like to say just a few more words about love, for once you finish your examination, I'll be out of your life. A student, sitting right where you're sitting now, asked me a question about love. It was about this same time last year. She asked me if I thought that I could ever entertain or experience the kind of idyllic love expressed by Mr. Shakespeare in his play, *Romeo and Juliet*..." Adena peeked into the open classroom. "I answered in the negative to that question. I would like to take this opportunity, in front of all of you, to retract that statement. Love is for all people, those who are old as well as young, and for everyone in between. It is there for every person to experience." Adena's face was glowing.

*   *   *   *

The topping of burley tobacco has been around since tobacco first entered the inter-national market, possibly even before. Topping tobacco is a process whereby the bloom of the plant or flower is removed before it buds or flowers. Once it flowers, the plant will use its resources to produce seed, and the size of the leaf will remain dormant. The buds removal before flowering causes the plant to concentrate on the leaves, the leaves increase in size, and the plant increases in mass.

People who worked in the fields topping tobacco wore standard topping regalia to protect themselves from excessive contact with the leaves of the plant, insect bites and, from the constant rays of the sun. The standard outfit for a topper usually required gloves, dark glasses, broad brimmed hat, long pants, long-sleeved shirt, and good walking shoes. The planter or the owner of the field provided the cutting tools, break areas with toilet facilities, and plenty of ice cold drinking water and water for washing hands. Every worker was also given a ten-minute break every hour.

As Mark and Adena stood at the edge of the tobacco field, Mark could have sworn that the field extended at least three miles to the horizon. The scene of the field and the nearly one hundred workers surrounding him made for quite a first impression.

The hot sun was beaming down, and the workers were feeling its effects. The actual work of cutting off the top of the tobacco was not difficult, nor was the rest of the work hard, but at about mid-day, the heat and humidity became almost unbearable. Also, the work was highly repetitive, making the work very boring by late afternoon.

On or about the third day in the fields, Mark stopped topping and looked around him at the people spread throughout the seemingly endless field. All of them that he could see were soaking wet with sweat, and he assumed that all of them were bored to death. Exaggerating the Southern dialect, Mark yelled out to the people around him, most of them college students, "Hey, everybody!...Ahh say...ahh say everybody! Give me your attention for just a quick moment!" Everyone in the vicinity stopped and listened to what Mark was saying, "Let's bring this field alive. Let's do something more than just cut, cut, cut, or...lift that bale and sweat, sweat, sweat. Let's bring a little class to this field of endeavor. Once upon a time, there was music in this field. Let's give music a rebirth. Everybody, join me, and let's fill this field with music. Let's do it to it. We can start off with that old classic, "Swing Low, Sweet Chariot"...and if you don't know the words, just hum along and drop the word Jordan and use Georgia!"

Adena thought at first that Mark had lost his sanity, but when he finished, she knew that he was pulling off another dramatic stunt, the kind of stunt that helped her fall in love with the man in front of her. "Say, Yankee? Are you becoming Southern fried?!"

They both returned to topping the tobacco and began to sing. Others joined in until everyone on Mark's topping crew was singing,

"Swing low, sweet chariot
Comin' for to carry me home!
I looked over Georgia and what did I see,
Comin' for to carry me home!
A band of angels comin' after me,
Comin' for to carry me home!
Swing low, sweet chariot,
Comin' for to carry me home."

The field came alive with song, and the singing continued until the "knock off work bell" resounded throughout the valley. For three weeks of topping, singing late in the afternoon, under the direction of Professor Mark Phillips, became a daily ritual.

*   *   *   *

In or around the latter part of June, the tobacco warehouses went into full production. Burley tobacco was for sale, and buyers came into Magnolia from all over the world. The Holiday Inn, for July and half of August, became international and overbooked.

Inside the warehouse were stacks of tobacco piled on top of large squares of burlap. Each stack came from independent farmers or from the farms owned by Tim Bremmer. When a bundle was purchased, someone would tie up the four ends of the burlap square and move it from the floor to the buyer's station. Each buyer had an assigned location within the warehouse where his daily purchases would be stacked.

It was Mark's job to move from one stack to another, and on a special form, he wrote down the winning bidder's number, the weight of the sack, and the winning bid. The bid price per pound was determined by the quality of the tobacco making up the stack. Following the winning bid, Mark would hand his completed ticket to Adena, who would accumulate a handful of completed bid tickets and run them into the office to be processed.

Huge circulating fans attempted to cool off the interior of the warehouse, but once the day moved into early afternoon, the warehouse would become a sauna. Most of the workers wore as little clothing as they could get away with and still be looked at as "decent." Needless to say, Adena, aside from the stack of tobacco being bid on, was the center of attention. Mark took the entire scene in stride. On a couple of occasions, he had to remind a few bidders that she was taken. The bidders, both male and female, but primarily male, wore business attire. The whole scene inside the warehouse was rather incongruous. The men were in suits and ties. However, in the early afternoon, and even on their return from lunch, their coats would be abandoned, and their ties would be removed or their tie knots would be hanging midway between their waistlines and their necks.

Another bothersome element about the warehouse was the abundance of tobacco dust floating in the air. At times, it became so bad that some of the workers would put on little white face masks. In the afternoon, the fine tobacco dust and the not-so-fine managed to find their way onto the sweaty bodies, and some faces took on the appearance of African or Indian carved masks.

Into this hostile milieu came the auctioneer. His auctioneering, at times, became almost melodic with the established rhythms, the cadence, the inflections on the numbers combined with such inserts as, "Do I hear?" "I have!" "Do I have?" and "Going…going…" The bid spotters standing beside the auctioneer helped to establish almost a poetic chanting quality, with their yelling, "Yep…yep…yes" every time some bidder met the bidding price set by the auctioneer.

The days were long, but they became a learning experience for Mark and Adena. They learned about a world that they had only heard about, and they learned rather quickly how to relax in a hurry once the day was over. Fast foods and frozen prepared meals were the order of the day.

Everything was going along without a hitch with no problems for either Mark or Adena except the haunting realization that Mark had not found a job for the fall. At the end of the fourth week in the warehouse, Mark and Adena left work after a typical long, hot day and headed for the car. "God! What a summer! I now fully appreciate an air-conditioned classroom."

"Come on, Yankee. Let's go to your apartment, and I'll give you a good old fashioned Southern rub-down, and if you're up to it, maybe even something else."

"That is the best invitation and expression I have heard all day."

Mark reached the driver's side of the car and reached for the door handle when his hands began to tingle, his feet became numb, and as at Tim Bremmer's pool, the world started to go around his car. His legs buckled beneath him, and his whole body embraced the earth. Adena ran around the car and tried to catch him before he fell, but she just couldn't make it in time. She braced herself behind him and raised him to a sitting position. He was not unconscious.

"Mark, what in the hell is going on? Are you okay?"

Mark saw the spinning world come to a slow stop. His body was limp, and his face wet with perspiration. "I don't know what happened, but my hands and feet went numb, and the next thing I knew was that my body lost its strength. It was like being hit by a giant vacuum cleaner and having every bit of my strength sucked out of me."

"Mark, why don't you go and see Will tomorrow? Your health insurance is still good until September first. You told me that yourself."

"I'm okay. I know I'm having a reaction to that intense heat and humidity in the warehouse today. I'm just worn out and extremely tired. Didn't I hear you offer me a rub-down?"

"Yes." She helped Mark back up and onto his feet. He was still a bit shaky.

"Let's get out of here." He handed her the keys. "You drive."

*   *   *   *

In the back of an exquisite bar located in the Peachtree Plaza, where candle-light was providing the only source of illumination, Paul Rutherford and his former wife, the mother of Adena, sat in conversation. "If Carl knew you were sitting here with me this afternoon, you'd find yourself in another divorce court."

The comment from Rutherford didn't even create a flinch. "He had to fly out to San Francisco this morning. I saw him off at the Atlanta airport. I thought that his departure would be a perfect way to kill two birds with one stone."

"Your implications are overwhelming me. You've always had a twisted sense of humor. Did you bring the papers?"

"I have them right here in my purse. Only before I hand them over to you, I want to know if you've taken care of my little problem."

"The word I received two days ago was that your dear Professor Phillips has no job, and his honorable status in the community has been destroyed. Seeing as how August is just around the corner, his chances of finding a job, from what I understand, are next to zero. His ex-wife has already served him papers warning him not to let his medical insurance lapse on his daughter."

"Very good, only I'm still worried about a possible October wedding."

"You don't think that Adena is stupid enough to marry someone who can't even support her, do you? My God, didn't she inherit any of your blood?"

"I'll let that ride. Adena thinks she is in love. And when someone is in that frame of mind, a person is capable of doing some crazy things."

Paul glanced at her purse and continued, "A possible wedding is your problem. I've done all that I can do. I've broken the man for you, and now I expect you to live up to your side of the bargain." He held out his hand, "The papers, please."

She removed them from her purse, "Here they are. I guess a thank-you is in order."

Rutherford was looking over the papers and didn't look up. "Not necessary. It appears that all the papers are here." He looked at his ex, and his eyes were piercing, "Remember, from this day forward, there are no more bonds between us." He stood up and walked away, leaving her sitting at the small, dimly lit table all by herself.

*   *   *   *

"Mark?..." She saw that calling his name was not going to work this morning, so she went to him and gently shook his shoulder, "Mark, honey. It's time to get up...I have breakfast cooking, your favorite, pancakes and a fresh cup of coffee. Mmmmm, doesn't that sound inviting?" She continued to rub his shoulder and his forehead. Mark opened his eyes.

"What do I see before me? I must be in paradise. An angel of mercy is attending my wounds. Or,..." He rose up on his elbow to take a closer look, "...is this Aphrodite before me, the goddess of love?" He started to laugh, "Quick, find me Hercules so that I might borrow some of his strength!"

"Mark, you're crazy."

"And you're beautiful." He reached up with one hand and started to caress one of her breasts.

"Hey! I don't see any Hercules around anywhere in this room." She got up from the bed, "No time for hanky panky this morning. We are already running a bit late. So, get your shower going, jump into your socially-accepted outer fixings, and come into the kitchen for breakfast." She jumped away from Mark as he attempted to grab her and ran to the kitchen. Mark slowly lifted himself out of bed, took a couple of steps toward the bathroom, reversed himself rapidly back to the bed, and fell backward across it.

"Adena!...Adena!"

Adena rushed back into the bedroom and ran to Mark who had managed to sit upon the side of the bed.

"My God, Mark! You're pale as a ghost!" Mark could feel Adena tremble.

"Hey, take it easy. I'm going to be all right. However, this morning I wish I were a ghost. That way I could float into the bathroom."

"What is wrong?" He knew by the tone of her voice that she was worried and concerned.

"All I can think of is too many hours in that hot warehouse and not enough sunshine." He attempted to stand and made it to his feet with Adena's help.

"I'll be okay. The world has stopped spinning around." He could feel Adena's body relax slightly. "Be sweet and bring me a cup of coffee into the bathroom. I'll savor it while I remove this stubble from my white face."

She slowly released his arm, saw that he could stand, and felt a bit of relief. "Okay,...but you call me if you need me."

Mark made his way into the bathroom, looked into his bathroom mirror, and knew immediately the cause of Adena's concern. He was as white as the chalk he used in his classrooms. Adena came into the bathroom and placed his cup of coffee on the back of the commode and moved to his side, "Please, Mark, for me if not for yourself, go and see Will this morning."

"From what I see in the mirror, you're absolutely right…I'll drop you off at the warehouse and pay my friend a visit." A smile came across Adena's face as she headed back to the kitchen.

"Thank you…My, God you're a stubborn…a stubborn…whatever!"

"When I see Will this morning, he will finish your sentence for you."

Mark could hear Adena laughing from the kitchen.

As they drove past the University, they could see that the new academic year was getting its head start. Rush had begun. The campus was overflowing with young students wearing their best fashions and others wearing their fraternity or sorority outfits. Adena glanced at Mark as they drove by, and not once did he turn his head. They finally arrived at the warehouse.

"Don't get out," said Adena. She jumped out and ran around to Mark's side of the car. He rolled down the window. "Promise me, now, that you will go and see Will."

"I promise."

"And let me know something as soon as possible. I'll be a nervous wreck until you do."

"You have my word." She gave Mark a quick kiss and ran into the warehouse.

CHAPTER 12

▼

"Ever has it been that love knows not
its own depth until the hour of separation."

Kahlil Gibran

Mark couldn't remember the last time he was in Will's clinic. At the moment, he had the realization that he should have been here a lot sooner. However, he thought, when one feels in the prime of health, why go to a doctor? Besides, if he had something bothering him, he would confide to Will either at his home or over lunch.

Mark had taken off the medical robe and was getting into his pants when Will walked in.

"Well, Doc, what's the verdict?"

"You should have come in for your physical when I told you to...You're a stubborn jackass." Mark knew that he was going to finish Adena's statement from this morning. "Finish getting your clothes on and come into my office."

"Ohh, ohh. That serious is it?"

"Do you have to be dying to come into my office? You happen to be my closest friend in this whole damn town. I tell you at least a dozen times to get your ass in here to see me, and what do you do? You have the love affair of your life. Now, get your damn clothes on and come into my office. We need to wait until your blood work and urine test results return from the hospital lab. And, as I can't give you a scotch and soda here or out in my lobby, my office is your only possible oasis."

"How come you have scotch and soda in your office?"

"Because I knew that, sooner or later, a certain jackass was going to walk into my office and, as usual, he would be thirsty." Will left the room, and Mark started to laugh.

✳   ✳   ✳   ✳

Mark was finishing off his fifth scotch and soda. Consequently, he had mellowed out considerably.

"How were the drinks?" Will asked as he looked over Mark's lab reports that had just arrived from the hospital.

"Well, I think if I had about three more, I would have some of the same symptoms I have been experiencing for the past two months."

Will smiled, shook his head, and continued to look over the reports. The more he read, the more his face became stern and serious.

"To tell you the truth, Will, I haven't been able to afford too many scotch and sodas this summer."

Will did not take his eyes off of the report, "Then why in the hell didn't you visit me more often?"

"I think love has something to do with it."

Will dropped the papers he was holding in his hand and moved from his desk to stand in front of Mark. "Your tests were not good, Mark. Your red blood count is way down...I'm not going to bullshit you or dance around the mulberry bush...You know me better than that. You need more tests, and you need them done in a better lab facility than I have at the local hospital."

Mark finally became serious. He knew that Will was not pulling his leg.

"Am I in trouble?"

"It's too early to tell, Mark. Like I said, you need more tests. And you definitely need some rest."

"On that score, I can agree with you one hundred percent."

Will reached over to the wall, pulled up a chair, and sat down to face Mark. He grabbed a note pad off of his desk.

"I need to ask you some very important questions, and no bullshitting around."

"Go ahead."

"Have you noticed any numbness or tingling in your fingers, hands, or feet recently?"

"I started having numbness in my fingers about four or five weeks ago. A few times, it was so bad that I couldn't type...I just tossed it off to muscular exertion."

Mark could see a very serious countenance come upon his friend's face. He knew better than to ask any questions. He knew that Will would give him all the information about his condition in due time, and didn't Will say that it was too early to come to any specific answers?

Will stood up. "Mark, I want to send you to Emory University Hospital in Atlanta. I want you to go this afternoon. I'll call ahead and arrange for a room to be waiting for you."

There was a long pause, "I can't, Will."

"What in the hell do you mean, you can't?"

"The health insurance that I had with the University has lapsed."

Will bent down and glared into Mark's eyes, "You're going, and I'm personally going to admit you...I want to be in on the necessary tests and involved in the final diagnosis." He crossed back to his desk.

Mark stood up from his chair, "Didn't you hear me, Will. I can't pay the damn..."

"Mark Phillips, you leave everything to me, and if you give me any arguments this time around, I'll whip your ass. In your condition right now, it wouldn't be much of a contest...I'll go out to my front desk and make reservations for us at Emory. In the meantime, you use my desk phone and call Adena."

Mark looked rather stunned, "What can I tell her?"

"My God! For a writer and a play director, your imagination seems to have taken a slump. Tell her you're going to Atlanta for a job interview." He started toward his office door.

"Thanks, Will...I..."

"Don't say another word. Just call." And with that comment he left his office.

Mark crossed to Will's desk and sat on one corner to make his phone call. John Rivers, the tobacco warehouse office manager answered the phone.

"Say, John, this is Mark...Mark Phillips. Listen, I need to talk to Adena...Can you call her to the phone for me? Thanks." Mark was still a bit stunned, and he was really wrestling with the idea that he was about to lie to Adena. As he waited for her to pick up the warehouse telephone, he heard a group of sorority and fraternity kids outside the office window passing by and talking about rush. Finally, he heard Adena on the other end of the phone.

"Hello! Is that you, Mark?" Mark reassured her that it was he and that he was checking in with her as he had promised.

"Hello, beautiful! This is your secret Yankee admirer calling."

"Mark, will you please get serious and tell me what's going on. I have been worried sick for most of the day!"

Mark cringed as he began his first lie to Adena, "I have two wonderful bits of news. The first one is, I'm okay. Dr. Will's diagnosis was that I was just run down and needed a little rest from the rigors of the tobacco warehouse." Mark could hear the change of mood in her voice.

"Thank, God!"

"Are you ready for this next piece of news?...I finally have a job interview at a college in Atlanta!" He was doing his best at giving a believable dramatic performance over the phone. Stanislavsky would have been proud of him. "I just now plucked the interview letter out of the mailbox."

"Fantastic!" Mark could see her dancing around with the receiver, "We'll do something special tonight to celebrate."

It was now time for an even greater voice performance, "That won't be possible, sweetheart. I have to leave right away. My interview starts first thing in the morning. It may take as long as two or three days because a few of the key people on the selection committee are out of town. Still on vacation, I guess. Anyway, I'll call you as soon as I get to Atlanta. Check with Joe at work. He lives just down the street from me, and I'm sure he won't mind driving you home."

"Good luck with the interview, darling. My prayers will go with you. I'll be waiting for your evening call."

"Until this evening...I love you."

"I love you, too."

Mark lowered the receiver back into its place and moved to Will's desk chair. He placed his head on Will's desk and wept. For the first time in his life he was afraid.

*   *   *   *

Mark was reading the <u>Atlanta Constitution</u> when Will, along with two other doctors, walked into his hospital room. "Good morning, Will, and the same to the rest of your entourage." Almost in unison they replied, "Good morning, Dr. Phillips."

"Will, I feel great. I looked in the mirror this morning, and my face looked normal." Will did not reply but turned to the other doctors, "This man is a personal friend of mine. If you all don't mind, I would like to talk to him alone." The other doctors nodded in agreement and left the room. Mark's jovial mood quickly went to pensive. "Okay, Will, what's the story?"

"You do know that you were sedated last night?"

"Yes."

"And, as you have already mentioned, you noticed an improvement in your skin color?"

"Yes…. yes…and yes! Will, will you tell me what in the hell is going on?"

"We gave you a blood transfusion last night."

"Okay, so what does that mean?"

Will crossed to Mark's bed and sat on its edge. "Mark, damn it, it's times like this that I dislike being a medical doctor." Will could see fear written across Mark's face. He continued, "And it's much more difficult when the patient is your closest friend."

"Will, you're talking to an ex-Marine and a friend of over ten years. Yes, from your demeanor, I'm scared to death about what you're about ready to lay on me, but I've been to the 'Iron Triangle' in Korea, so give it to me straight and fast!"

Will tried his best to stiffen his back bone and to control his emotions, but tears flooded his eyes, "You have a very advanced case of primary aplastic anemia."

Mark's face went blank. "What in the hell is that?"

"You don't need to know, but you do need to know that you have, at the most, two months of life to live." Will shot up off the bed and crossed to the window. His emotional control was completely lost.

Mark bolted upright in bed. The <u>Atlanta Constitution</u> went flying everywhere. "Will, you've got to be kidding?!" Mark felt like his throat just had a noose pulled tight around it."

"I wish I were," replied Will.

When Mark got his voice back, he asked again, "You've got to be kidding, Will?!"

At the nurse's station down the hall from Mark's room, they could hear his cries of agony, his repeated shouts of disbelief, interspersed with the name of "Adena!…Adena!"

*   *   *   *

The next day, Mark and Will were standing outside Emory Hospital, getting ready to make their return trip to Magnolia.

"Mark, you must be back here within three days. You know that don't you?"

Mark was very subdued, "Yes, I must return in order for the folks in there…" He pointed back to the hospital, "…to prolong my life a few extra days…or weeks."

"Do you want me to tell Adena?"

Mark went from subdued to almost violent, "No!…I must handle this in my own way!" Will started moving toward his car in front of the hospital. Mark grabbed him by the arm, "Will, you must promise me, you must give me your solemn word that you will not mention anything about this to Adena. And I beg you not to tell her where I am!"

Will took Mark into his arms and held him tight, "God damn it, Mark, I know what you are going through. I deal with death a least every month of the year. You have my solemn promise that nothing will ever be said to Adena."

They both climbed into Will's car and departed Atlanta.

*　　*　　*　　*

North Georgia had received a few near-freezing nights early in September. The trees in Mark's Garden of Eden, as elsewhere around Magnolia, had outdone themselves in producing their colorful last lease on life. Mark held a special bond with his trees on this day of days, for today he would have to give the performance of his lifetime to an audience of one, an audience that he loved more than life itself.

Early that morning, he had paid a visit to his attorney to make sure that his will was up to date. He added Adena along with his daughters to share in his land. He also called Adena at the warehouse. The only words spoken to her before he hung up the receiver were, "Meet me on my land at one o'clock this afternoon."

When they met, the curtain opened, and Mark began his performance. Adena jumped out of the car she had borrowed at work and ran to Mark. He embraced her and held her in his arms. Somehow, at least in his own mind, he absorbed within him, a part of her spirit. He then held her back from him and simply said, "We must talk."

He dropped his hands and began to walk in the direction of where they had discovered the watermelon a year ago. Adena was stunned. The embrace left her feeling abandoned, cold. She couldn't understand why there was no kiss, no romantic rapture. She was totally shocked as she followed Mark into the forest. They walked for what seemed hours but were only minutes with no holding of hands, no laughter, no warmth, and nothing but silence. Only the natural sounds of the forest could be heard. Finally, Adena could no longer take the silence, "You didn't get the job?" She stopped on the path, but Mark continued to walk. "Damn it, Mark Phillips!" She started chasing after him, "For the love of God, will you speak to me?!"

She ran around in front of him and blocked his way. He finally stopped. "You call me from Atlanta or wherever and tell me to meet you here. I follow your directions, we embrace, and all you have said to me is, 'We have to talk'. Aside from the embrace, you haven't so much as touched me—it's like I had the plague or something." Adena, bewildered, frustrated, hurt and angry, rushed at Mark and began pounding on his chest, screaming out into the forest, "Will you speak to me…Speak, damn you!…" Mark grabbed her hands and looked her square in the face. His hands were beginning to tingle.

"I want to break our engagement."

Adena's mouth dropped open. She could not believe what she had just heard. Mark released his grip on her hands, and she stepped back from him.

"Do you know what you just said to me?" Tears were beginning to show in her eyes. In Mark's mind, all he could hear was, "The show must go on!"

"Our engagement must come to an end."

"Why? Because you didn't get that job in Atlanta?…To hell with the world of academia. We, you and I, can make it together. I cannot believe what is happening or what you are saying." She stood in front of him like a lost child, "Mark…I beg you to hold me."

"I can't. I can't." He shook his head and walked past her. She followed him, feeling like she was walking in some kind of nightmare.

Adena shouted at his back, "If you had or have any love for me at all, Mark Phillips, please, please explain what in the hell is going on. What is happening!"

Mark turned to confront her, "I simply discovered within the last few days that society is right. Your family is right. Everyone is right, and we are wrong."

Adena was still totally perplexed, "What are you talking about?…Society?…My family?"

"Our age difference, that's what I'm talking about!"

Adena moved her head up and down slowly. Finally, she thought that something made sense, not much sense, but it was better than nothing. She moved a few steps toward Mark.

"There is no age difference between us as far as I'm concerned. You…"

"But there will be, Adena. And that aging process is occurring now."

"Mark, something happened in Atlanta?! What? What has come over you? You just don't end a love like ours in the passing of a second or on a damn trip to Atlanta!"

Mark knew that he was about to give the final soliloquy of his performance. His strength was fading fast.

"Adena, listen to me. You're in your early twenties and I'm forty-five. My hair is getting grey around the ears. The grey will spread and soon, like my late father, my hair will become snow white. You see these wrinkles around my eyes? They will increase until eventually they will conquer my face. My flesh will start to sag and fall. It will become sickening to the touch." Adena started to reply. "No!" Mark shouted, "Don't speak! Let me finish! When you're at your sexual prime, I'll be at my sexual decline. Between thirty and forty, you'll burn with human desire, a desire that I will not be able to fulfill. In your thirties, you will begin to think about the life you didn't have a chance to live. Our love, the love we have now, will sicken and rot like a withered peach upon the ground. I should never have allowed it to happen."

Adena could not hold back any longer. Her anger was reaching the point of no return. "Damn it, Mark!" She moved closer to him. "Have you listened to what you're saying? Do you think I'm stupid? Do you think I haven't thought about all that you've said here this afternoon? I didn't fall in love with your flesh, nor did I fall in love with your hair or your penis. How can one fall in love with those things?! They have no heart, no spirit, no soul! I fell in love with those three things and what comes from them. Dear, God, Mark…can't you understand that I care nothing about those things you talked about?!"

Mark could feel his legs going numb. The feeling had already left his hands. The curtain was about to close.

"I'm sorry, Adena. It's over." He moved past her and started walking back towards his car.

Adena shouted after him, "Mark!"

He stopped for just a fleeting second and then continued walking to the car.

Adena shouted again, "Mark!…I love you!" Her words seemed to echo through the forest and pierced into Mark's back and into his heart, but there was no turning back.

Adena fell to the ground and wept.

Mark got into his car and drove away. Not too far from the main road leading back to Magnolia, Mark turned off onto an old side road and traveled on it for about a half a mile, going as fast as his old Falcon could travel. He slammed on the brakes, turned off the car, jumped out, and ran to the side of the road, and looked up into a beautiful, clear, blue autumn sky.

He raised his fist up towards the heavens and shouted out into space. "God?…Do you hear me?!" The volume of his voice increased with every word, "The one thing I have been searching for all of my life—you allowed me to touch for just a fleeting moment—and then took it away. If I could yell louder than Job—if I could pierce the very gates of heaven with my voice and my thoughts, You would condemn me to Hell!"

Like Adena earlier, Mark fell to his knees and wept.

*   *   *   *

A heavy "norther" was moving south across Georgia, bringing with it freezing temperatures at night and chilling winds during the day. The sky was bleak, and not a cloud was in the sky. The weather, in general, was exactly the opposite of the previous year.

No Indian summer days this time around. When fall rushed in, it seemed like it was seeking some kind of revenge, some paid tribute for the year before.

Adena was standing by the campus lake, in her and Mark's favorite spot. She was wearing the thickest winter coat that she owned. A lonely figure standing in the wind, her hair was down, blowing and billowing in different directions across her face and back.

Suddenly, out of nowhere, she heard her name being called. She recognized the voice immediately and swung around to face her oldest sister, Delores, running across campus in her direction. Adena broke out of her trance and raced to meet her. They crashed in an embrace. Adena could not hold back her joy at having her sister present. The emotions that she had been holding back for the last three days erupted onto her sister's shoulder. When her emotions subsided, she managed to speak.

"Dear, God! Dear, God! I'm so glad you're here. I didn't think you would come. I thought…" Her tears once again took control, and she couldn't speak.

"I got the note that you left on your apartment door. Don't cry, Adena. My, God, I'm sure that in the last few days you have cried enough to last a life time."

They walked over to the lake and sat at one of the picnic tables. As they sat down, Adena started to shake her head, "You don't know. You don't know what…"

Delores reached out her hand and placed it over her sister's. "All I know is what you told me over the phone, and that was enough. Besides, when you called, I was packing and getting ready to come up here."

"Why? You were coming to see me?" Again she broke into tears.

"I have something very important to tell you. But let's find a warmer place. I'm about to freeze to death. When I left Albany the temperature was in the 70's." They both got up from the bench and, with arms around each other, started walking across campus.

Adena's apartment was as sparse as her checking account. Tim Bremmer had given her a full-time job for as long as she wanted it and was certainly willing to do the same for Mark if he didn't land a teaching job. However, she had used all of her savings to make the necessary deposits and to purchase the meager furniture that she now owned. Her table consisted of a crate turned upside down, covered with a piece of cardboard and a coverlet of fabric. Two bean bags served as chairs. They were both occupied as Delores related a taped conversation that she had accidentally listened to between her mother and their biological father. Their mother apparently taped the conversation between her and her former husband when she went to hand over the papers that would have incriminated him with the IRS.

Delores, wanting to record some music while visiting her mother, knew that she had a small recorder somewhere in the house. She found it, saw the tape inside, and started playing a portion of it to see if it was blank. What she discovered sickened her to the very marrow of her bones. She related all of the conversation to Adena and told her that she had made a copy of the tape if it was ever needed.

Adena's face was white with anger, "I can't believe it!...I just can't believe our mother could be so cruel...so evil...so, so destructive of another human being. Poor Mark." She leaped up from the bean bag and started to pace the floor. "They stripped him of his dignity and pride!" She swung violently around, like she was trying to shake something off her back, and faced her sister, "I have never, never felt like killing someone, until this evening." Delores didn't say a word. She simply gave her sister time to vent her anger and her hurt.

After pacing and screaming obscenities and threats against her mother for what seemed like hours, Adena finally collapsed into her bean bag.

Delores reached across the gulf that separated her and Adena and placed her hand on her arm. She was afraid to ask the question that was on the tip of her tongue, but she also knew that it had to come out sooner or later. "Sis? You told me over the phone all about what happened between you and Mark and now, you must tell me what you wouldn't tell me over the phone. I think I already know what remains, but you need to let it out."

Buried halfway into the bean bag and facing away from her sister, in a fetal position, with a voice barely audible said, "I'm...carrying Mark's baby! I found out the same afternoon that he left."

Delores left her beanbag, crossed to her sister's, and found room beside her. "My, God! How much you have suffered for falling in love. Adena...Adena, listen to me." She snuggled down into the beanbag and put her arm around her sister. "You must find Mark and tell him about the baby, and about what our mother and father tried to do to him. Listen to me. You must do this." Adena could not cry any more. Her tears were exhausted. She did hear the words of her sister, and strangely enough, all of a sudden, she could see a ray of sunshine at the end of a very long black tunnel.

Delores stayed with Adena for three days, helping her to locate Mark. She felt like her presence gave Adena strength and one other person that she could confide in and hold onto in a world that looked very bleak and lonely just one week ago. The first place that they went to was Mark's apartment. As Adena was knocking on the door, a neighbor appeared and told her that it was useless to knock. A moving company had pulled into the driveway yesterday and emptied the place. He also informed her that neither he nor the other neighbors had seen Mark within the last couple of weeks.

Adena went to the dean's house, and once again, he was outside working in the yard. She inquired about Mark, asking the dean if he knew where he was, or if he knew whether Mark had obtained a teaching position at another college or university. Had he received any phone calls from Mark? The Dean could only answer in the negative and was no help in her quest to locate Mark. Delores, trying to help, went to the U. S. Post Office and had the postmaster check all of the recent changes of address. No forwarding address could be found for a doctor, professor, or Mr. Mark Phillips.

Adena drove out to the Bremmer mansion and talked with Tim. Tim told her that the last time he saw or heard from Mark was the day before he took off work in order to go to Atlanta. Tim was very concerned because what was happening was totally incongruous with the Mark Phillips he had known for ten years. He also was worried about Mark's sudden disappearance. He contacted the state vehicle department and had Mark's tag number traced and then phoned the state police to notify them that the owner of the tag number was missing. Adena, before departing, gave Tim a kiss on the cheek, thanked him, and promised to let him know right away if she learned of any new information or…found him.

Adena did not want Delores to leave, but she understood that she was needed back on the farm. It was the main harvest time of the year, especially the pumpkin crop, and Delores's first allegiance was to her husband. Adena could not thank her sister enough for coming into her life when it seemed like life had come to an end. She had her strength back, and the life within her gave her the resolve to live, no matter what the consequences.

After Delores drove away, it dawned on Adena that there was one person, one place that she had not checked. She could have kicked herself for not thinking about him sooner. Before Delores left, she had gone to the Avis Rental Car Company and rented her a car for as long as she needed. She also gave her her credit card to use as long as was necessary. Adena jumped into the car and drove to Dr. Will's clinic.

She entered his office and brushed right by the receptionist. She caught Will coming out of one of the examining rooms, and at the same time, Will saw her approaching. The oath that he had made to Mark came flooding back.

Adena grabbed Will by the arm. "Will, do you know where Mark is? I have been searching for him for the last week, and no one,—I mean no one, knows where he is and, no one has seen him in a week. As far as I know, you were the last one he saw before leaving for his job interview in Atlanta."

Will thought to himself, "May God forgive me for the things I'm about to say."

"Adena, all I know is that I gave Mark a clean bill of health. He told me that he had a job interview down in Atlanta and that it sounded promising. I suspect that is where he is, and he is probably quite busy, seeing as how the fall semester was just about to begin when he left." Will gritted his teeth as he saw all hope drain from Adena's face. "While you're here, you might be able to help me. Mark told me about Regina's appointment to a prep school for West Point. He never gave me an address or a phone number. I would like to send her a congratulations card. Might you have her address or phone number?"

Adena's mind was whirling. She knew that if this man didn't know where Mark was, no one would. Wasn't he Mark's best and closest friend? As she moved back down the hall, she told Will that maybe, just maybe, she might have Regina's phone number somewhere, but that she would have to look through some unpacked boxes back in her apartment. She made Will promise that if he heard from Mark, to please let her know right away. When she left, Will told his nurse to cancel and reschedule the rest of his appointments, and he secluded himself in his office for the remainder of the day.

Inadvertently, Will had given Adena a ray of hope. The first thing that she did when she got home was to look for Regina's phone number. She knew that she didn't have her address, but on the day that Regina had arrived at her new duty station, she made a call to Mark. Mark didn't have a thing to write with, so he had Adena write the phone number down on a scrap piece of paper. When she got to her apartment, she went through everything, and in one of her old purses, she found one piece of paper with a phone number scribbled on it. Her heart leaped, but she wasn't sure it was the number that she had spent the afternoon searching for. Anything was worth a try.

She dialed the number, and finally something positive occurred. Someone answered the phone and sounded off about barracks so and so, and rank so and so. Adena immediately asked to speak to Regina Phillips. As soon as Regina came to the phone, Adena quickly filled her in on what had happened between her and her father. She even told Regina about her pregnancy. Regina's initial reaction was total disbelief. She could not understand her father acting the way that he had. Something else besides the age issue prompted his actions. Adena filled her in on Mark's physical problems and ended her conversation with, "You must take emergency leave!"

Regina replied, "Why?"

"Something's happened to your father. My sister and I have searched the whole town, and we can't find him. Everything's gone from his apartment and no one who saw the moving truck paid enough attention to it to notice the name. Dr. Will and Tim Bremmer haven't heard from him nor have they seen him in over two weeks!"

"Are you telling me he doesn't even know you're pregnant?!"

"Yes."

"I'll see you first thing in the morning." The phone went dead.

CHAPTER 13

▼

"Your pain is the breaking of the shell that encloses your understanding. Even as the stone of the fruit must break, that its heart may stand in the sun, so must you know pain."

Kahlil Gibran

Dr. Westmore's receptionist opened the front door, and Regina rushed in, still in her West Point uniform. Adena was right behind her.

"Adena, wait here in the lobby," Regina said, "I'll be right back." She opened the door that lead back to the examination rooms and ran directly into Will.

"Regina! My, God, I'm glad to see you!"

Adena heard Will talking to Regina behind the door. She moved quickly to the hall entryway so that she could hear what was being said.

"I've been trying to reach you for the last couple of days. I tried getting your number from the West Point Academy, but everyone I talked to was military idiots. No one knew that you were attending the academy." Will did not know that Adena was on the other side of the door. "Adena came into my office yesterday, and I even asked her if she knew how I could get in touch with you."

Regina could detect an urgency in Will's voice, "Dr. Will, you're scaring me. What's happened to my father? Adena told me you don't know where he is. I can't find anyone who does know." Regina's voice kept getting louder and her gestures more frantic. "It's like he just vanished from the face of the earth!"

"Regina...Regina, calm down." He reached out and gently laid his hands on her shoulders, "I can explain." Adena moved closer to the door. "You must leave Magnolia at once and go directly to Emory Hospital in Atlanta!"

Adena burst through the door. "What are you saying, Will?! You told me yesterday that you didn't know where he was but presumed that he was in Atlanta...and now, Emory Hospital?!"

"God forgive me, Adena. Mark begged me to promise on my oath that I wouldn't tell you where he was or what had happened to him."

At this point, Adena lost complete control. Screaming, she lunged at Dr. Will. Regina intercepted her and held her back from plowing into Dr. Will's chest with her flailing fists. "Damn you, Will!...Damn you!"

Regina yelled out over Adena's shoulder, "Will, you can tell me. I'm not Adena!...Tell me what is happening to my father!"

Will looked at Regina and for several seconds said nothing. Tears welled up in his eyes, and for the first time in his entire professional life, he openly wept as he told her that her father and his dearest friend was dying. Both Regina and Adena stood frozen like ice statues. Both appeared as though someone or something had cast a spell upon them. Will continued, "Your father has an advanced case of primary aplastic anemia. His bone marrow is no longer capable of producing red blood cells." Will's next comment was the most difficult to utter, "There is no cure…. Also…."

Regina pulled out of her stupor, "Also?!…What is the also?!"

"…four days ago he started developing a heart dysfunction."

Regina grabbed Adena, almost pulling her off the floor, and headed to the clinic entrance. Dr. Will shouted to her, "Wait," She spun around and looked back at Dr. Will. "Three days ago I called Tim Bremmer, and he told me how to contact your sister, Salina, in Singapore. I contacted her, and she gave me the number of your sister, Theresa. They both should be at the hospital when you get there. I will call Emory and tell them that you are on your way."

"Thanks, Will." With that statement, she and Adena disappeared out the front door.

*   *   *   *

Speed limits didn't apply to Regina as she drove out of Magnolia and headed toward Atlanta. As the miles whipped by, she and Adena entered into some intense conversation. Adena asked Regina not to say anything to her father about her pregnancy. Regina didn't agree, but Adena was adamant. "There is no other option. Please promise me you won't say a word. Just remember what he and I have gone through these past months. If he's going to die, I want him to go with his mind at peace."

Regina understood this reasoning and promised her that she would not mention anything about his child.

As they sped along the highway, Adena's hand clamped on Regina's forearm so hard, and suddenly, Regina almost lost control of the car.

"That exit up ahead leads to your father's land. Regina! I want to go there for just a moment. I know just where I want to go. I beg you. Please. I promise you, on my life, that It'll only take a minute."

Regina took the exit.

*   *   *   *

Hospitals are all the same, and Emory Hospital was no exception. They attack the senses. The sounds are the same; most look the same and smell the same. They are even mystical to a certain extent. Within the confines of their walls, life is saved or terminated. There is sickness and wellness, joy and celebration, tragedy and lamenting. There would be a death here tonight, but in just a few months, a birth would even things out.

Theresa and Adena sat on either side of Regina, on a couch in the intensive care waiting room. Regina had her arms around both. The on-duty nurse entered the room. She was under the impression that all three girls in the waiting room were Mark's daughters. "Your father is out of sedation now, but his condition is very weak. He suffered a mild heart attack earlier this morning. You can go in and see him, but please be very brief. I know what you're going through. I lost my dad two years ago, but we must think of the patient first and foremost."

Regina took her arms from around the girls and stood. "Thank you."

The nurse left the waiting room and returned to her duty station. Theresa and Adena stood. All three looked at one another. Adena was the first to speak. "Go, both of you. I want to see him alone, if only for a minute." They nodded, walked down the hall to their father's room, and entered. They both moved close to the bed. Regina placed Theresa in front of her. Both, almost in unison spoke, "Dad?"

Mark slowly turned his head toward them. He smiled when he saw who was standing by his bed.

"Two of my angels. His voice was very low but clear. "Regina, let me look at you in your uniform."

Theresa moved aside, and Regina came forward and managed a very weak turn.

"What a sight for a dying man." Regina started to say something, but Mark interrupted her, "Don't. I'm going to die. It's alright, we all do it you know, sooner or later."

Regina summoned all of her learned stoic military demeanor and said, "I love you, Dad."

"I love you too. And I'm so damned proud of you."

"Theresa, come closer. And get those tears out of your eyes; they spoil your beautiful face." Theresa moved as close as she could to her father's bed.

"I regret that," He reached out and gently put his hand on hers, "I never had much of an opportunity to be a guide in your life. We never had a great amount of time together."

Theresa managed to get her reply in between sobs, "You've been more of a guide than you realize." She bent over the bed and kissed his cheek. "I love you."

Regina tapped Theresa on the shoulder and pointed toward the door. "We need to leave for a short while Dad. The nurse told us we could stay only a few minutes. Besides, there is someone else to see you. We'll be back soon." They quietly moved to the door and disappeared into the hall.

Mark watched them move toward the door, and in the dim light of his room, saw them exit. The light from the hall pierced the darkness and blinded his eyes for just a fleeting second. He closed his eyes, and when he did, Salina appeared to him in his mind. Her smile was radiant as usual. Without hesitation, Mark mentally and emotionally reached out and pulled her into his arms. Her last words before departing for her sailing adventure became loud and clear, "Most of all, Dad, I love you for all the love and trust that you have given me through the years...and also for your faith." Mark's yearning to see her before he died was intense.

As her image began to fade away, other images began to fill his mind. Pictures appeared, and they were as clear as projections on a silver screen. Mark was standing beside his father, holding aloft his first fish. The next vision was his mother putting on his first band-aid, kissing his scratched knee and in her soft reassuring voice, telling him that his hurt would soon go away. He felt her pull him in close to her and her warmth engulfed him.

The images were coming fast and furious. Mark smiled, his academic, analytic mind was telling him his suitcase was being packed with memories to take on his journey of no return. He had come to the acceptance of the inevitable.

Pictures of love and softness gave way to pictures of maimed bodies, bullet-ridden flesh, and cries of agony. Mark's body shook in reaction to the vivid memories of the bitter ice and snow, the freezing temperatures, and to the suffering of his marine comrades somewhere on the hills of Korea.

Quick, still pictures of the births of his daughters crowded out those of death and suffering. Pictures of his various graduations, from high school to the doctorate zoomed past his eyes.

His mind went blank. Pictures and visions disappeared into a mist; sounds took their place. Various musical sounds came into Mark's ears, and he felt like he was in the middle of a full symphony orchestra as each instrument was warming up for a grand performance. The notes immediately flooded together, and the music of his beloved composer, Rachmaninoff, seemed to lift him above his hospital bed. As the music wrapped around him, he could see an object joining him as he floated along with the music. When he recognized the object, the music dissolved immediately. Above him, moving in slow motion, was a hawk. With recognition of the hawk, Mark's body returned to the bed, and words that he thought he would never hear again soared into his suitcase of memories, "Someday, I want to be as free as that hawk!" Mark always associated those words with the first day he began to fall in love with Adena.

The memory gate stayed open, and they began an invasion into Mark's thoughts and emotions. His senses became acute to the onslaught of the pictures, sounds, and smells confronting him. He saw the fireworks of joy in Adena's eyes when he gave her the engagement ring.

The aromas of Italian cooking filled his nostrils, and his mouth began to water. Along with the aromas came Italian music so real that Mark thought that the Italian musician was standing right next to his bed.

He saw Adena descend the stairs in her antebellum gown, and he felt their bodies move as they glided across the gymnasium floor to Rachmaninoff. He felt her hand in his as their sweat soaked bodies moved through the fields of tobacco. He felt the pressure and movement of her body as they christened, by their act of love, his small parcel of paradise.

His suitcase was now filled, and yet his soul felt empty. He wanted his universe to grant him one last wish, but he knew that it would be impossible. He wanted to see the woman he loved one last time. One last time.

An explosion of light momentarily filled Mark's room and pierced Mark's closed eyelids. The light brought him back to the real world. He heard the soft click of his room's door as it closed. The light disappeared as quickly as it had appeared. Someone had entered. He opened his eyes and strained to see through the darkness. Someone was standing just inside the door holding something in front of her.

"Salina?" asked Mark.

"No, Mark, not Salina."

Mark immediately identified the voice. He lifted himself onto his elbow and looked at her. "Adena! No!…I don't want you here. I didn't want you to see me this…" Mark knew his voice betrayed his lie.

Adena interrupted him as she went to his bedside, "I knew you'd be pissed off, you big jackass, so I brought a peace offering." She held it out so he could see the object in her hands.

A huge smile lit Mark's face, "Is it...it is! Another watermelon fall!"

"Yes, it's another watermelon fall."

As Adena placed the small watermelon on a tray-table near Mark's bed, Mark rested back on his pillows. She removed a nail file from her purse and cut the small melon in half. Realizing that time was short, she used her fingers to quickly remove two small pieces of the watermelon's heart. She put one piece gently into Mark's mouth. Holding her piece in her hand, she said, "This watermelon is a symbol of our love for one another. Eating it, as we did once before, will join us together until we meet as one in paradise." They ate the melon.

Mark felt a tingled sensation ripple through his body, and a sharp pain surge through his left arm. He knew another heart attack was imminent. As he silently fought his pain, Adena leaned across the bed, kissed the man she loved, and embraced him. Concealing his inner pain, Mark gently pushed Adena away and looked her up and down, and said, "Are you gaining weight?"

"That is a helluva thing to say at a time like this." They both smiled.

Mark's pain was becoming intense. He knew he had to get Adena out of his room as quickly as possible. Fighting to keep his pain out of his voice he said, "See that manuscript on the window sill?"

"Yes?"

"I want you to finish my book."

"But...Mark?...How can I finish your book?"

"You can because what it seeks, we lived."

Adena crossed the room to the window sill and picked up the manuscript. Its cover was purple and it felt like soft velvet. She started to cross back to the bed, but Mark raised his hand, palm up, and stopped her. What strength he had left, he used to raise himself up on one elbow. When he began to talk, Adena knew that what he was saying was sincere and a plea for her total understanding.

"My beloved, Adena. My last wish was granted that I see you, we've been blessed with the opportunity to say goodbye. I know you can finish my book. I want you to take it and go. I don't want you here with me when my life ends. Please. I want you to remember us the way we were and not as we are now. Go, and promise me you won't come back to this room for any reason. Do you promise?"

Adena held his book up to her breast and said, "I promise."

As she crossed to the door, Mark said, "Please ask my daughters to come to my room." Adena paused at the door and over her shoulder said, "Salina should be here at any moment. She's flying in from Singapore." She left the room and closed the door behind her. As she made her exit, Mark painfully lowered himself back down on the bed.

Adena slowly walked down the hall toward the elevator with her head down. Her sense of hearing seemed to be working overtime. Every step she took sounded like a hollow echo reverberating from a deep cavern, and with each step forward, came the temptation to run back to Mark's room, but her promise kept moving her forward. Her tears were leaving small black spots on the cloth covering the manuscript.

Her first stop was in front of the visitor's waiting room. Without looking in or turning her head, she cleared her throat and said, "Your father wishes to see you now." She could hear the girls rushing down the hall as she continued toward the elevators.

When she passed the nurse's station, she managed a weak smile and a nod to the nurse behind the desk. When she stood in front of the elevator, she heard a wail; the hallway became a megaphone. Adena knew that the cry of lament came from Regina and the wail pierced her heart. As the elevator door opened, she turned to see the on-duty nurse running down the hall towards Mark's room.

The elevator made slow descent, Adena held Mark's manuscript tightly against her. His book seemed to give her strength, and she knew that Mark Phillips would be with her forever.

She stepped off of the elevator and to her total surprise, she saw her mother and her stepfather in the lobby. She went straight to her mother and stood in front of her like a marble sentinel. Adena's eyes turned icy as she glared at her mother. She said nothing. Her mother had to break the unbearable silence.

"Adena!...Following your call to Delores just before you left Magnolia, she called us and told us about Mark's being here. More importantly, she told us, with some prodding, about your condition. We knew that we would find you here. I think it's time for you to come home."

Adena was surprised to see tears in her mother's eyes, something she had never seen before. Adena's hands tightened around Mark's manuscript as she continued to glare into her mother's eyes. She could find no words. Her thoughts were simply of pity for what she saw standing in front of her. Her mother was talking, but no words fell on Adena's ears as she turned and slowly walked to the front door of the hospital. She could hear only her mother yelling in the background.

"Adena!...Adena!...Forgive me, Adena!....I'm...."

It was raining outside, so before she left the protection of the canopy, she stuffed Mark's book under her jacket and started to walk out into the storm. A taxi pulled up in front of her, and a girl jumped out of the cab. Adena knew from pictures that it was Salina. The rain, falling on the canopy was drowning out all sound, but Adena made an attempt at getting her attention.

Adena called out to her, "Salina?!" Salina paid the cab driver and quickly glanced in Adena's direction. No recognition took place.

She watched Salina rush into the hospital, and in a low voice, as she turned to continue her walk, she said, "You're too late…In this life, most everyone is too late."

Adena disappeared into the rain.

The End

EPILOGUE

▼

Dad, I can't leave such a beautiful love story on such a down note. Consequently, I must tell you a few more things even though you already know. When the truth became known about what my grandmother and grandfather Rutherford tried to do to you, the people in Magnolia also became aware of mother's condition. Many of your students, townspeople, and your colleagues at the University, along with Barry (Salina's husband) and his dad, raised money to build a wonderful log cabin on your property, right next to where you and Mom found your first watermelon. I was born in that cabin, and a few hours after my birth, Mom joined you, in…wherever.

Today, when life gets ugly, unbearable, or stressful, Regina, Salina, Theresa, Aunt Delores, and I use the cabin as our personal retreat. Your earthly paradise is still beloved.

Life works its own miracles. Aunt Delores couldn't have children, so when I was born and Mom left, Aunt Delores inherited a healthy baby girl.

And, Dad, I will finish your book.

The Beginning

978-0-595-35603-4
0-595-35603-6

Printed in the United States
32889LVS00006BA/94-510